TWELVE TWISTS OF FATE

A collection of short stories by

Bob Goddard

Timbuktu Publishing

Published by:

Timbuktu Publishing, Stables Bungalow, Mill Reach, Buxton, Norwich, NR10 5EJ, UK

www.timbuktu-publishing.co.uk

ISBN 978-0-9563518-5-2

British Library Cataloguing in Publication Data available.

Cover by Destiny Productions
https://www.facebook.com/destinyproduct/

CONTENTS

This book is dedicated to my wonderful wife Viv,
who makes the tea and mops my fevered
brow while I write

CHAPTER 1

Distant Memories

"My house, my *house!*" yelled Reuben, as the Volvo turned into the driveway.

"Yes, it's ours for the week," said his mother, Sophie, turning towards the back seats with a puzzled smile. "A holiday in the country where we can all just relax and have fun."

"But it's my house, *my* house," he insisted, waving his six-year-old arms excitedly.

"Oh, no," said Chloe, one of his older sisters, "he's having one of his funny moments."

"Let's hope he doesn't *wet* himself again!" said Phoebe as she and Chloe collapsed in fits of giggles.

"Please," said their father, as he brought the estate car to a halt on the gravel, "can we just pretend that we're a normal family? At least until the owners have gone. Look... here they come now."

A middle-aged couple wearing welcoming smiles appeared at the top of the steps leading from the front door. “Hello! Hello!” they said.

“Welcome to Doulton House,” said the woman.

“Your home for the week,” said the man. “You’ll love it here,” he added with an ingratiating grin.

Sophie was first out of the car, walking up the three stone steps to shake hands with the couple. “This is lovely,” she said, as she took in the roses growing over the mock-Grecian front porch. “I’m Sophie... and this is my husband, Ben.” He rounded the front of the car and trotted up the steps. “Our daughters, Chloe and Phoebe...” She gestured towards the twin girls who had emerged from the car and were scampering in the gravel driveway, hand in hand.

“And our son, Reuben.” She turned back to the car, where the young boy had stopped waving his arms and legs and was now open-mouthed, staring through his round glasses at the house. “I’ll go and let him out.” Sophie opened the door, unclipped his straps and encouraged him out of his seat.

“Say hello to Mr and Mrs Briggs, Reuben.” She held his hand while he skipped to the top step.

“Hello,” he said, dutifully, pushing his glasses up his nose and squinting up at the house’s bedroom windows. "My house," he added, raising his arm towards it, a large purple birthmark visible beneath his chin.

"Yes, young man." Mrs Briggs smiled down at him. "That's right. It's yours for the week. Come along and I'll show you and your mum around."

She led them to the open front door while her husband went to help Ben lift cases from the back of the Volvo. Before they reached the doorway, however, Reuben wriggled free from his mother's hand, and pushed past Mrs Briggs.

"*Reuben!*" scolded his mother, but he ignored her and ran inside. The two women stopped on the threshold as the boy ran down the wood-panelled hallway waving his hands at the doors he passed, singing out, "toilet, lounge, study, parlour, utility, kitchen." He stopped at the end, turned and grinned at them.

"Oh, I'm *so sorry*, Mrs Briggs!" Sophie said. "Reuben gets a bit excited sometimes."

Mrs Briggs turned to her with wide eyes. "How *on Earth* did he know? Have you been here before?"

"Um, no... never." Sophie looked at her son in exasperation. "He does sort of... guess things, sometimes." She saw he was now squeezing the front of his shorts. "And I think he needs the loo. Reuben! Toilet! Now!"

The lad scampered back up the hallway and into the door to their left. His mother pulled the door shut as they heard the toilet seat crash against the cistern and an urgent tinkling began.

"Sorry. It's been rather a long journey." She smiled an apology.

Benjamin Collier stood at the bar while the landlord pulled him a pint. The Rose and Crown was quiet this early in the evening, the Saturday diners and drinkers still out enjoying the August sunshine.

"And a bottle o' wine to take out, you said...?" The landlord placed the glass of foam-topped liquid in front of him. "What sort d'you fancy?"

"Do you have a Shiraz?" Ben asked, craning his neck to read the bottle labels on the shelf behind the bar.

"Certainly do, Squire." He reached for a bottle and handed it over. "'Ow's that suit yer?"

"Yes, thanks. That'll do fine." He took a long sip from his beer, then by way of explanation, said, "My wife's cooking supper. We're staying at Doulton House, just down the road."

"Oh yeah? Doc Morrison's old place. Lovely 'ouse... shame about what 'appened."

"What... erm... what *did* happen?" asked Ben, taking another draught from his glass.

"Prob'ly shouldn't say. It being a posh holiday home now. Was a while ago, anyway..." The landlord picked up a glass and polished it with a tea towel, waiting.

"No... go on, what did happen?"

"Killed 'isself, poor old Doc Morrison did. Discovered 'is wife was 'avin' it off with the gardener. Couldn't deal with it, so he topped 'isself..." the landlord lowered his voice and leaned over the bar conspiratorially, "wiv 'is shotgun."

"Bloody hell!" Ben spluttered into his pint.

"Yeah, a right mess. His wife found 'im in the green'ouse, or what they called 'The Orangery', 'cos they was posh, like."

"Crikey!" Ben took another swig from his pint, eager to hear more and eager to get away at the same time. "Must have been a while ago," he said, "there's no greenhouse in the garden now."

"Oh, it's still there," said the landlord, "only it's hidden behind a fence now. 'Arf the garden's been fenced off by the new owners—"

"Is that Mr and Mrs Briggs?"

"Yeah. They bought it last year. Tarted up the house and front 'arf of the garden, but left the old green'ouse and the bottom of the garden to run wild, they 'ave. Can't say I blame 'em. Helluva lot o' garden at Doulton House. Thass why poor old Doc Morrison 'ired a gardener in the first place. Dangerous thing you know... too much money."

He went off to serve another customer, while Ben assimilated the information and made an instant decision – he would be telling none of this to Sophie. He laid a twenty-pound note on the bar and sipped the last of his pint while he waited for the landlord to return.

"Thank you, Squire." The landlord laid a surprisingly small amount of change on the beer mat. "Hope you 'ave a nice holiday. And don't forget to treat the missus..." He winked at Ben.

"Erm... treat her... how?" Ben instantly regretted the question, fearing the answer might be some appallingly crude rustic witticism.

"By bringing 'er in for a nice meal!" smiled the landlord. "Save 'er doing the cooking. She's on 'oliday too, right?"

"Oh! Yes! Right. I'm sure we will, um, pop in for a meal. But we have three children too, so... perhaps somewhere out of the way?" He scanned the bar area for a nook where the children, Reuben in particular, might eat without causing too much embarrassment.

"Back room... quiet as yer like," said the landlord, gesturing over his shoulder with a thumb. "Want me to book you in, Squire? Then you can have the room all to yerselves, in case it gets busy..."

"Come on Doctor Reuben, come and make us better," jeered Chloe in a sing-song voice as she pranced around the garden, just out of reach of the boy who chased after her.

"Come on Doctor Reuben, my leg is broken and I can't run," called Phoebe, limping theatrically, only to dash away when he tried to grab her.

It was the 10-year-old twins' favourite game, baiting their younger brother and teasing him mercilessly over the odd things he'd said. Like declaring he was a doctor, a claim they'd made him regret every day since he was five. And then suddenly he wasn't chasing them anymore, but was running through a gap in the hedge, heading for the fence beyond.

"What's so special about this old fence, Reuben?" Phoebe caught up with him as he trailed his fingers along the larch-lap planking.

"Not old. New fence," he said and continued walking beside the towering barrier.

"New fence then. You can't get past it, you know—"

"There's a lock on the gate." Chloe finished her sister's sentence for her.

He ignored them both and stumbled onwards to the wooden gate. He reached up to the padlock and twiddled with the numbers that rotated beneath his fingers.

"You'll never get in, Reuben," said Chloe. "You need to know the secret code, and nobody knows that—"

"Only Mr and Mrs Briggs, and they're not here," said Phoebe. "Why d'you want to go through it anyway, Reuben? It's only old weeds and jungle through there. Daddy said so. Full of spiders and snakes and horrible creepy crawlies, I expect." She made a mock spider with her hand, and ran it up his neck and over his scalp. Reuben squealed and pushed her away.

"Come on Doctor Reuben," sang Chloe, pulling on his arm. "Come and chase us again."

"It's Doctor David," he mumbled, "not Reuben." He continued to turn the numbers on the padlock.

"Ooeeoo! Doctor David now, is it?" said Phoebe. "Come and chase us then, Doctor David, or the spiders'll get you!" She tickled his neck again.

"No!" He shrugged her off. "I need to get through..."

"Doctor David, Doctor David... spiders gonna get you!" sang the girls as they both joined in tickling him. Which made him shriek and stamp his foot with frustration. Then he felt a familiar sensation. The girls left him at the gate and ran back through the gap in the hedge, across the lawn to the house, shouting delightedly: "Mummy, Mummy... Reuben's wet himself again!"

"There you go, Squire," the rotund landlord of the Rose and Crown handed Ben a sheaf of menus, "kiddies' meals on the back. I'll send Kaffy through to get your orders in a minute, alright?"

He smiled and nodded at the Collier family who were seated around the back room table, then shifted his considerable weight to his other foot, ready to return to the bar.

"Hello, Chris!" called out young Reuben. The landlord turned to the lad, who was squinting up at him through his round spectacles.

"'Ello young man. Yeah, everybody knows ol' Chris."

"Have you got my Tullochmore?" said Reuben. The table fell silent and everyone stared at the boy.

"Cor! They got you well primed, ain't they, lad?" said the landlord. "We ain't 'ad Tullochmore since poor old Doc Morrison did 'isself—" He stopped short when he saw Ben's deep frown and sharp shake of the head.

"I 'spect a coke is more up your street, young man." He smiled at Sophie, but she wore a shocked and puzzled expression and didn't respond. "I'll get Kaffy to come and get yer drinks."

As he shuffled off back to the bar, Sophie turned to her husband. "Why did you tell Reuben the landlord's name was Chris?"

"I didn't! I didn't know it myself until just now!" he protested.

"And what's all this Tullochmore and Doc Morrison business? You must have got very *pally* the other night..." She looked at him sharply.

Ben heaved a deep sigh. "Look, I'll tell you later. Let's just enjoy a meal out for once without..." He looked up gratefully as the young waitress approached with pad and pen. "Ah! You must be Kaffy?"

"No. My name's Kathy." She sniffed and jabbed her biro in the direction of the bar. "'E can't talk prop'ly, silly old so... sausage." She sniffed again. "So... what yer wanna drink?"

Sophie sat stiffly on the edge of the settee as Ben placed a mug of cocoa on the coffee table in front of her. "Look. I'm sorry about the Rose and Crown. I really didn't know it would be so grim. I thought you would appreciate a break from cooking, it being our last night and all that."

"Oh, well. Never mind," she said. "These country pubs can be very hit and miss. Just hope we don't all go down with food poisoning." She looked up at him and patted the settee beside her. "Now come and sit down, Ben, and tell me what this Tullochmore and Doc Morrison is all about – something you were discussing with that oafish landlord, obviously?"

He sighed and sat down beside her. "I have *absolutely* no idea where the Tullochmore came from. It's a rare Scotch whisky, but where Reuben heard about it I don't have a clue. And how he knew the landlord's name, I have no idea." He patted her knee. "You know what he's like, Sophie. He just comes out with these extraordinary things someti—"

"What about this Doc Morrison," she asked impatiently. "You were keen to stop the landlord saying any more about him."

Ben sighed again. "Look. I didn't want to tell you. An unfortunate incident connected with this house. I didn't want to upset you and spoil our holiday."

"We're going home tomorrow, Ben. I think you'd better tell me."

"Well, okay then. There was this Doctor Morrison, and this was his house. Apparently he discovered his wife was having an affair with the gardener. He couldn't cope with it and went down to the greenhouse at the bottom of the garden and committed suicide... that's all."

"That's *all!*" She looked horrified. "How did he do it... with a garden trowel?"

"Shotgun, apparently."

"Oh, God! That's awful, Ben. When was this?"

"I don't know. A few years ago. The place stood empty for a while until the Briggs's bought it last year and did it up... well, at least the house and top half of the garden. They left the greenhouse –

or Orangery as it was called – and the bottom end of the garden to run wild. Just put up that great big fence beyond the hedge to keep people out."

"I can imagine. I thought there was something strange about this place. It's obviously upsetting Reuben too. I'm pleased we're going home tomorrow."

"Right, Reuben," said his mother, "you can play in the garden for half an hour while I finish packing. Your sisters are playing in their bedroom, so you've no reason to get upset today. Keep those clothes clean, because that's what you'll be wearing to travel home in, okay?"

Reuben nodded and skipped down the steps to the driveway. This arrangement suited him just fine. He had a plan. Ever since breakfast he had been itching to try it out.

On the front of Doulton House, high up between the bedroom windows, was a stone block with writing on it. Reuben was convinced it held the answer. He ran out across the gravel circle and turned to look up at it. The sun was high overhead as it was almost lunchtime, and Reuben couldn't make out the words and numbers in the glare, even when he scrunched up his eyes and wiggled his glasses around. Not even when he folded his fingers around his eyes and squinted through the gaps.

This was disastrous. He had been certain the solution he needed was written in stone, high up on the front of the house. It had come to him in a flash of inspiration as he munched on his Rice Krispies, and he'd been trying to contain his excitement all morning. But it was no good. No matter how hard he stared, the vital information on the stone tablet was unreadable. He sat down in the gravel in resignation and sank his head into his stubby little fingers.

And suddenly... it came to him. He knew what it said – 'Doulton House, 1935'! Reuben scrambled to his feet and dashed around the side of the house, across the lawn, through the gap in the hedge, and along the fence until he came to the gate. He grabbed at the padlock and turned the little numbers until they read 1935. There!

He pulled on the padlock, expecting it to spring open, but nothing happened. He frowned at it, pushed his glasses up his nose and jiggled the numbers to make sure they lined up exactly. 1935. He was sure that must be the answer. Nothing. The hasp stayed locked firmly in place. The gate stayed firmly shut. The fence stayed firmly impassable.

"Boggit!" he yelled. It was the worst word he could think of. He went and found a stick and used it to hit the padlock over and over again until the stick snapped in half. He sat down on the damp grass and moaned at the unfairness of it all. Beyond the fence was an answer – *the* answer – he felt sure of it. He kicked at a caterpillar that was crawling past, but it didn't make him feel any better.

Slowly, he got to his feet, brushed the grass and ants off his legs and stared defiantly at the padlock. It stared defiantly back. 1935 it said. He lifted the heavy metal lump to see what it said on the other side. 5379. But that wasn't right. What if he was looking at it from the other side?

Reuben struggled to turn all four numbers at once, so the 1935 appeared on the other side of the padlock. His fingers fumbled a few times but finally, if he held the lock upside down, it read 1935 on this side. He pulled at the hasp, but nothing moved. "Boggit!" he squeaked in frustration.

Then a thought occurred to him. Maybe the numbers had to line up, not on the front side, or even on the back side while upside down, but at the bottom of the lock. He twiddled the numbers and finally the last one clicked into place at the bottom... and the padlock sprang open with a click.

"Yes... Boggin' YES!" His legs danced a little dance without him asking them to.

With trembling fingers he swung the opened hasp up through the hole in the metal plate on the gate and dropped the padlock on the ground. Then he pulled the hinged bit aside and the gate swung inwards. He slipped through into a world of head-high nettles, brambles and creepers, stopping to look for creepy-crawlies among the dark shadows. Then he began to pick his way through the undergrowth towards the deepening gloom of the overhanging trees.

Reuben only stopped once. He looked back through the vague sort of tunnel he'd made and could just make out the wooden fence. Then he turned forward once more and pressed on, deeper into the jungle. There was something... a shape... a window. As he pushed aside a large clump of nettles that stung his hand and made him say 'Boggit' several times, he finally saw there was a row of windows and just off to the right, a wooden door with glass in.

After beating a path to the doorknob, he wrapped his sticky fingers around it and turned until it went click and the door jerked open. He gave a push and, with a squeak of hinges and a small blizzard of paint flakes, the door slowly creaked open. Inside were several small trees, some of them with dark green, glossy leaves reaching up to the glass roof, some of them dead, their dry branches strung with cobwebs.

He knew this place. It had been in his dreams forever. It had caused him countless nightmares and wet pyjamas. But he had to step inside. Somebody made him do it. Her name was Angela and she was with someone else. She was his wife and she was in here with... the gardener!

Consultant surgeon, Doctor David Morrison, had something heavy in his hands and he was going to scare that bloody gardener out of his wits. He could clear off and never come back.

But the gardener had grabbed the twin barrels of the shotgun and he was strong. Much too strong. They struggled with the gun as Angela cowered amongst the orange trees. Then he felt the cold metal underneath his chin...

An ear-piercing scream split the hot summer afternoon. It tore through the tangled undergrowth, raced across the lawn and rattled the elegant windows of Doulton House. Ben dropped the case he was loading into the back of the Volvo and looked up in time to see his wife sprint out of the front door, around the side of the house and disappear, closely followed by his two daughters. He set off after them.

Ben caught up with his girls just inside the gate that had miraculously opened in the tall fence. They were standing on the edge of a jungle of brambles and nettles and creepers, too scared to follow their mother who had blundered onwards. He could hear her shrieks as the thorns and nettles tore at her skin. He could also hear her calling, "Reuben, Reuben... hold on darling. Mummy's coming."

Ben plunged into the undergrowth after her and soon came to a crumbling structure that had once been a grand greenhouse – The Orangery! He pushed open the broken door to find his wife on her knees at the far end of the musty building. She was holding something small and soft, and she was moaning. "Reuben, Reuben, Reuben. What were you *doing* in here?"

Ben ran to them fearing what he would find. Over his wife's shoulder he could see Reuben's eyes blinking rapidly. He'd lost his glasses. "Reuben! What the hell—?"

"Shhh!" hissed Sophie. "He's trying to tell me something..."

Reuben stopped blinking and looked up at them. "He killed me, Mummy. The gardener... he killed me dead."

Ben crouched down and kissed his son on the forehead, then lifted him up from the floor.

"Look Ben!" gasped his wife. "Look – his birthmark's gone!"

CHAPTER 2

Freedom

The axe cleaved the cold air, flashing in the brittle sunlight, arcing downwards.

CLUMP!

"Damn!" Morgan cursed under his breath. The log hadn't split. Instead it held the axe-head fast in its knotty fibres.

He straightened with a groan and looked across the dusty yard to the log cabin. Tendrils of blue smoke wisped from the chimney and the heady scent of fruit pies baking drifted on the breeze. He wiped the back of a grimy hand across his mouth hungrily and squinted, but she was hidden inside her domestic fortress.

Near the fence, laundry billowed, his shirt's sleeves writhing in a futile bid for freedom. Beyond it their chestnut stallion stood motionless by the corral gate, its neck taut, eyes fixed on the distant hills.

But there could be no escape. Not unless something were to change.

Morgan reached down and pulled on the hickory handle, but the axe remained stubbornly embedded, trapped in the wood's tenacious embrace. With a rising growl he hefted both axe and log high into the air and brought them down with a pent-up howl.

The log split clean in two. The axe fell free.

"Yeah," he smiled to himself. "That would do it."

But it would have to look like an accident, or better still, like someone else did it. He mopped his brow with his bandana and reflected on last month's Sioux raid in the north of the county. He thought about the old Indian bow and arrows hanging on the wall in the barn. The hitching posts at the back of the cabin would be perfect. All it needed was some twine and a trigger...

Morgan smiled again, reached into his shirt pocket and stroked his lucky silver dollar.

Morgan scooped the last spoonful of apple pie into his mouth, chewed and swallowed. "There's a beautiful moon tonight," he said with a grin. "Thought I might take you outside to go look at it."

"Really?" Elizabeth looked up in surprise, then smiled. "That would be nice."

"Leave the dishes. Let's go see it now." He pushed back his chair, stood and reached for her hand. With his other he felt his shirt pocket, but the silver dollar was gone. No matter. He'd have plenty of time to search for it tomorrow.

As they turned the corner at the back of the cabin, Morgan released her hand and walked behind her, holding her waist. "There," he said, pushing her toward the Moon. "Ain't that just the prettiest sight?"

"Oh look!" she cried, stepping forward and bending to pick a shiny, Moon-shaped object out of the dust.

A thought struck Morgan at the same time as the arrow.

Luck could be a fickle mistress.

CHAPTER 3

The Lone Yachtsman

Sophie Marshall giggled with embarrassment as her boss's hand slid up her leg. Whether it was the wine that made her titter, or the surprise of his meaty fingers inching under her skirt, she wasn't sure. But she knew if she played her cards right she might be in for early promotion, so she held her breath and let him explore.

What an end to her first week at Siskin Plc! The evening had been a blur of exotic food and expensive wine. The Dolce Lusso on the outskirts of Exeter was way beyond Sophie's salary, but Mr Setchford hadn't balked at the prices. Now, as they sat in his Range Rover in the restaurant car park, she supposed it was her turn not to flinch. Just as his fingers reached her knickers and Sophie felt distinctly uncomfortable, he withdrew his hand and she exhaled with relief.

"What say we pop to my little pad for a nightcap?" He smiled and raised one shaggy eyebrow.

"Um, okay then. But I mustn't be too late." She felt squiffy already. "I need my beauty sleep."

"Don't worry, my dear. You'll be in bed before you know it." He sniggered, thrust the vehicle into gear and revved the engine.

As the Range Rover shot forward over the loose gravel, she grabbed the door handle and gasped. But it was Mr Setchford who made the strangest noise: "Wha...gluck!"

He was silenced abruptly by a loud bang from the car roof. Sophie turned to look but he'd gone. And something warm and wet was spraying over her. And then she was screaming.

Detective Inspector Mark Plumstead was tired and angry. His weekend golf trip to Royal Porthcawl had been torpedoed. Instead, he had been awake since midnight trying to question an hysterical secretary and a bereaved housewife. All because a randy businessman had been decapitated in a particularly unusual and gruesome way.

"Bring me some coffee – strong coffee – not that muck from the machine," he growled, thrusting his chipped mug at DC Andrews. "Then we'll go over it again. We must be missing something."

The incident room dry-wipe board was criss-crossed with lines and scribbles. On the left side was a list:

1) Jealous Boyfriend
2) Enraged Wife
3) Angry employee
4) Pissed-off Business Partner
5) Family or Friend

"I think we can discount the boyfriend," said Andrews. "The Marshall girl insists she hasn't had one since last year and he's buggered off to Australia anyway. Her parents are in there now, trying to calm her down and get some sense out of her. Maybe she will reveal something to them that she hasn't told us."

"Who's our ears?"

"Evans, Sir."

"Okay. What about Mrs Setchford?"

"She's distraught at losing her husband. I think it's genuine. She says he's had flings with girls at work before, so she's not surprised. I can't see her sneaking into the car park and rigging his car up with a garrotte, Sir. I don't think she'd hire a hit-man either. If the secretary is to be believed, this was her first night out with her boss, so the wife wouldn't have had much time to get enraged, Sir."

"Bugger. I liked the idea of his wife doing him in. Angry employee, then?"

"Loads of potential there. He was a right bastard, apparently. Bought up companies, fired half the staff, made the others work their balls off. Then stripped the assets and flogged 'em on."

"So, how many might have had a motive to top 'im?"

"Oh, blimey. Five companies under his control at the moment with 197 staff..." He referred to his notebook. "And three flogged last year, four the year before that. There's probl'y five hundred who'd've liked to do 'im in, Sir."

"Fuck it, Andrews. We can't interview five hundred."

"No, Sir. Unlikely any of them would feel strongly enough to plan something like this, anyway."

"Business partner, then?"

"He has two co-directors with shares in Siskin, but they wouldn't have anything to gain by knocking off the chairman. His wife says his death will be the end of their gravy train, so I can't see a motive there, Sir."

"Family or friend, then, Andrews? Which of Brian Setchford's loved ones finally had enough of 'Mister Nice-Guy'?"

"Hard to say, Sir. We'll have to interview them all, I s'pose. His wife doesn't think there's anyone with a particular grudge."

Daniel Nesbitt swung the hire car into Windermere Car Rentals parking lot and sighed with relief.

"See!" Simon was gleeful. "Told you we would get back here without being challenged."

"No thanks to you." Daniel was exhausted by the drive from Bristol back up to The Lake District.

"We're a team," said Simon. "You're the driver – I'm the brains. And it worked perfectly, didn't it? 'Bristol businessman decapitated' said the radio news. You'd never have thought of the wire through the sunroof without me, would you?"

Daniel sank his head into his hands. "Just stop it, Simon. I don't want to think about what we've done."

"Well I'm pleased. That nasty old bugger had it coming. And nobody can catch us now."

Daniel wasn't so sure. He had covered their tracks carefully, but he knew a tiny shred of evidence could still catch them out. The latex gloves, roll of masking tape and reel of cotton were in a bag weighted with stones ready to be slipped into the water when he got out to the middle of the lake.

He dropped the car keys through the rentals office letterbox, shouldered his rucksack and strode towards the Windermere ferry in the early morning sunshine. The walk gave him time to think over what they'd done, and why.

Five years as Finance Director of Siskin plc had made him a witness to ruthless greed. He'd been shocked and dismayed at the plight of the sacked employees, but something made him stay. That something had been his partner Karen and their Victorian terraced house in Clifton. The mortgage was crippling but Karen loved the place. So Daniel turned a blind eye to the darker side of Siskin so he could keep his job, keep the house and keep his girlfriend happy. He fudged the figures and cooked the books year after year as his conscience sagged under the weight of it all. And finally, tragically, his doing nothing had cost him everything.

"Dammit, Andrews!" DI Plumstead's frustration was beginning to boil over. "Somebody must have had a soddin' motive. What have we got from forensics?"

"Nothing so far, Sir. No prints on the car other than himself and the secretary."

"And the wire?"

"Well, it's a length of sailor's rigging wire." Andrews consulted his notebook again. "Four mil', one by nineteen, Sir."

"In *English*, Andrews. I'm not Moby soddin' Dick."

"I think that was the whale, Sir."

"*Or* Captain Ahab, smartarse. I'm just a teensy bit *irritable*, Andrews, so I'd advise you to get to the point, or you'll be back on the beat."

"Yes, Sir. It's a four-millimetre stainless steel wire made up of nineteen strands. Forty feet long and fairly old. Commonly used to hold up the masts of yachts, but also used by the construction industry for stairways, walkways, suspended canopies – that kind of thing."

"So it could have been used anywhere... for anything?"

"Almost, Sir."

"Great. And can't forensics find anything on it at all? Useless bunch of wa—"

"They're running more tests now to see if

they can pinpoint where it's come from, but no human skin or hair on it, other than the victim's. The killer must have known Brian Setchford left his car's sunroof open on warm summer evenings. He used masking tape to hold a loop of the wire up inside, stuck to the headlining. The wire passed under his headrest, out of the sunroof and other end was shackled to a concrete fence post. When the victim drove away the wire spooled out, the loop dropped over his head like a noose and then bang, he was decapitated, Sir. Quite ingenious, really."

"Okay, then Andrews." DI Plumstead checked his watch. "I've been here since midnight and can't think straight. I'm going to get my head down for a couple of hours. Give the girl and the wife one more grilling in case they're hiding anything, then let them go. If nothing else comes up we'll have to start interviewing family and friends. And the employees. It'll be someone who knows him well enough to have a grudge. I'll be in cell five. Don't wake me unless you get a breakthrough, or I'll have your balls for earrings."

Daniel Nesbitt had soon discovered his boss was a philanderer. He'd seen Brian Setchford's love nest listed in the accounts as the company's 'off-site meeting room'. But the bills for champagne and bed linen identified its true purpose and it sickened him. So many secretaries, young and impressionable, had passed between those sheets. Some stayed a while, believing the weasel words and promises, but most soon realised they were being used and quit. It wasn't his place to challenge his boss's morals, so Daniel kept his thoughts to himself and shrugged off Setchford's lechery. It was none of his business. Not until the last Christmas party.

The annual office do had been a disaster. The festive food upset his stomach and Daniel was delayed in the toilets. When he returned to the dance floor Karen was pushing his boss away.

"Take me home. At once!" She fumed.

That night their little Victorian terrace shook with her fury. "He assaulted me! We were dancing and the next minute his hand was in my knickers. When I protested and pushed him away he said: 'You know you want it and I have just the place we can go'. Can you *believe* it, Daniel? Your own boss, Mr Setchford!"

"Yes," he'd replied quietly. "I can believe it. The man's a menace."

That's when he'd told her about the secretaries and the secret apartment. Big mistake. Then she wasn't just mad with his boss, she was angry with Daniel too. How could he have *known* all this time and never told her? How could he work for such a monster who abused innocent women? Daniel's hiding of the evidence in the accounts made him complicit – almost as guilty as Setchford himself – in Karen's eyes.

She locked herself in the bathroom and sobbed. Nothing he said would console her. After a Christmas week of agonising silence she announced her New Year's resolution. She was leaving. Daniel was devastated but felt sure she would come back. She adored their cosy little home, after all. And one day, in late January, she did return. She came with a man and a van and took all her things.

That was when Daniel's life-long companion, Simon, started nagging him to do something. He should find a way to stop Brian Setchford ruining people's lives. Permanently. His alibi could be his annual sailing holiday in the Lake District. Over the next few months Simon had convinced him that his plan was fool-proof. Finally Daniel had given in to the constant goading and agreed to carry it out.

A week ago he'd boarded his small hire yacht on Lake Windermere after making a point of parking his car right outside the charter company's office and leaving them the keys. Then he'd snuck round the back of the boat sheds where he knew an old yacht mast lay. It took less than a minute to unshackle one of the mast's wire stays. A stroll into Bowness produced the gloves, tape and cotton and a booking for the Ford from Bowness Car Hire.

Yesterday, he'd moored his sailboat on the far side of Windermere and swum ashore with his clothes in a waterproof bag. A short stroll south brought him to the ferry for a 10-minute crossing to Bowness where his hire car was waiting. Today, as he stepped back off the ferry, he was only minutes from the sanctuary of his little yacht. A lone sailor with a troubled mind.

"You *see*," Simon hissed in his ear, "I told you so. We will soon be home and dry."

Maybe I should start taking my medication again, thought Daniel. Simon was becoming less of a companion, more of a liability. No need for his nagging voice, now the deed was done.

"Andrews! Bring me some strong coffee and good news."

"Ah, there you are, Sir. Hope you slept well?

Nothing much to report except some scraps of fish scales forensics have dug out of the wire."

"What about 'em?"

"Well, apparently they come from the Arctic char, Sir. DNA testing shows these ones are found only in fish from the Lake District."

"*Is that so?* Fancy a little holiday, Andrews...?"

CHAPTER 4

George's Bottle of Wine

Old George's cheeks glowed as he remembered his day trip to the nearby Norfolk coast, and especially the restaurant in Cromer, where he'd been treated to lunch.

"Luvverly grub it were, and a relly noice bottler woine," he said. "Roger, the woine was called. Or Re-orger – suthin' loike that. It were a Spanish 'un."

His granddaughter Sasha smiled. "Oh, you mean Rioja? That's a Spanish wine."

"Noo, noo, that def'nly hadda a jay in it."

"That's right, Granddad. Jay is pronounced kay in Spanish. So it's called 'Ree-okka'."

"Well, thass a rummun, ennit? Jay pronounced *kay*? Why carn't they talk proper, loike oi dew?"

CHAPTER 5

Faintly Familiar

"Half a kilo of mature Cheddar, please." Rachel pointed to the pale yellow block behind the glass front of the deli counter. "And a quarter of Brie." She smiled at the girl in the white trilby and overall who was serving her. It was partly out of politeness, partly at the mouth-watering thought of the creamy, tangy French cheese. She could almost taste it now. Matthew would make his Cheddar last all week, but she knew that once she got her teeth into the Brie, it would be impossible to resist. That's why she only bought herself a small wedge. It would be gone in three days, but her waistline would benefit from the abstinence.

"A quarter kilo of Brie, please." Rachel's ears pricked up and she turned to see who it was who shared her good taste. But the woman placing her order with the young man behind the counter had her face turned towards the olives. She shuffled along with a limp and Rachel recognised her as the annoying shopper who had impeded her progress down the aisles earlier.

She shouldn't be impatient, especially with someone hindered by an obvious disability, but Rachel was a creature of habit. She liked to arrive at her local Waitrose at 8am prompt on a Saturday morning, to beat the start of the weekend rush. She would be loading her weekly shop into the back of her Nissan Juke by 8.45am and be leaving just as the car park started to fill up. The last thing she needed was to be stuck behind some 'Gimpy Gertie' who insisted on parking her trolley precisely where Rachel wanted to go.

That was another bad habit, making up mocking names for people she didn't know. Rachel mentally slapped her own wrist and leaned forward to order—

"And a quarter of Kalamata olives, please," said the woman, finger against the glass.

Rachel stopped herself from uttering an oath, and instead told the serving girl, "Oh, that'll be all for today, thanks." She picked up her wrapped cheeses and pushed her trolley away in silent fury. She loved those olives, but there was no way she could ask for them now. It was simply too embarrassing to appear to be copying the limping woman. She would go without.

Rachel completed her trolley dash at a frantic pace, determined to avoid another confrontation. She stuffed groceries into her Bags for Life at the checkout and dropped them into the trolley before opening her purse to fish out her credit and store cards. It was only then that she saw her olive-snatching rival queuing behind her and took in her face properly for the first time. The limping lady had a slightly odd look, as if her features might have received plastic surgery as some time in the past. But there was something faintly familiar about her too.

Rachel forced a smile as she folded the long till receipt and stuffed it into her purse. "Enjoy your olives," she said, with only a hint of malice, and set off for the store exit.

Why did the woman look familiar? Rachel thought back to last Saturday, when she'd encountered Gimp – *must stop calling her Gimpy Gertie* – the lady with the limp for the first time. She had followed the exact same route around the store then too, but Rachel had a head start and managed to avoid trolley rage on that occasion. Had she seen her face then and simply remembered it today?

Oh well, there was no danger of bumping in to her next Saturday. Rachel and her husband would be aboard a plane bound for Sardinia and a week's walking holiday. Gertie could have Waitrose to herself and stuff herself stupid with Kalamata olives, for all Rachel cared. She would be dining on the real thing in the land where they grew them. Sipping a cool Vermentino under a pergola of grape vines. Helping Matthew unwind and relax. Her job as solicitor's clerk was stress-free compared to his Sales Manager role at Cambridge's main Nissan dealership.

"Oh! Not her again!" Rachel hissed to Louise over the table at Manikins. "I swear that woman is following me!"

"Who?" The young redhead lifted her mouth from her coffee cup.

"Just came in the door, Lou." Rachel swivelled her eyes and tilted her head slightly.

"What... the woman with the limp?"

"Yeah. Been following me around the supermarket on Saturdays. Everything I put in my trolley, she put in hers. Everything I ordered at the deli counter, she ordered the same." That wasn't quite true, Rachel knew, but it suited the peeved way she felt at the moment.

Louise's eyes widened theatrically. "Oooh, Rachel. That's a bit spooky! Do you think she's stalking you... like in that film... whatsitcalled...?"

"God! I hope not."

"I think I've seen her before, Rach..." Louise took a sideways glance at the woman who had limped her way to a table by the window. "Yeah, I have. Coming out of McCall Ellis—"

"The solicitors!?"

"Yeah. For sure. Recognise that limp anywhere. I go down Clarendon Road on my way home. Seen her several times recently. Must knock off same time as us."

"You mean *she* works in a solicitor's office *too*?" Rachel was aghast. "That really *is* spooky! Hello, who's this...?" She nodded again, this time towards a smartly-dressed young man who had just joined the mystery woman at her table. He sat and laughed at some joke she had told him.

"That's Blake Ellis. He works at McCall Ellis too," said Louise. "Junior partner or something. His dad's one of the owners. Looks like he's chasing after the lady with the limp..."

"He won't have to run too fast." They both sniggered. "She moves at a snail's pace. I should know, I've been stuck behind her in Waitrose enough times."

"Oh well. You won't be stuck behind her tomorrow, Rachel. You'll be winging your way to the Mediterranean. I'm very jealous. Where is it you're going again... Sicily?"

"No, don't be so silly – *Sicily, geddit?*" Rachel liked to joke with her younger colleague. It helped break the tedium of formal letters and legalese that ruled their working days. "I'm going to Sardinia, Lou. A week of sun, sea and..." She winked at her friend.

"Oh my God! I hope your Matt knows what's expected of him." Louise giggled again. "He thinks he's going for a week of rest. You'll be bringing him back totally shagged out!"

"Shhh! Don't tell everybody." Rachel decided their conversation had turned a bit too saucy for the refined atmosphere of Manikins. Besides, the lady with the limp was looking their way and Rachel had hoped to avoid eye contact. Too late, she was staring right at them.

"She's looking this way now, Lou." Rachel leaned forward conspiratorially. "She's giving me the creeps. I'm sure I've seen her somewhere before. But I'd know if I had… from that limp, right?"

"Oh, forget about her, Rach. You've got better things to think about." She raised and lowered her eyebrows twice. "So what are you giving Matt for dinner tonight… oysters for aphrodisiac and fillet steak to build his strength up?" She giggled into her coffee cup.

"Probably. He's taking us to The Moorings for a pre-holiday evening out. It's expensive though. I just hope he doesn't blow his wad in the restaurant… Oh my God!" They both burst out laughing hysterically.

Luton Airport was not very inspiring at the best of times, but at seven on a Saturday morning it was dismal. Rachel felt queasy and uncomfortable about the imminent flight. It might be due to the Coquilles St Jacques she ate at The Moorings last night. If they'd called them scallops and charged a less fancy price, would they have been more digestible? Or maybe it was the Prosecco. She'd drunk most of the bottle because Matthew was driving. A breathalysed sales manager was an ex-sales manager he'd told her, as he sipped half a glass and topped up hers repeatedly.

Oh well. In three hours they would be in Sardinia and she could detox on the Mediterranean diet and a week of walking in the sunshine. Their resort hotel looked fabulous in the brochure and...

"I don't *believe* it!" Rachel gasped and grabbed Matthew's hand.

"What!?" He looked alarmed. "Don't tell me you've forgotten the passpor—"

"No... it's that *woman*! Look... just come through the departure gate." Rachel stared at the passenger hobbling along with a cabin bag on wheels. "It's Florence Nightmare – The Lady With The Limp. The one I told you about... who's been stalking me."

"Don't see how she could stalk you. Not very fast on her feet, is she? And hardly inconspicuous, either."

"You don't understand, Matthew. She works in a solicitor's office, just up the road from me. She shops in Waitrose at the exact same time as me every week—"

"So why don't you go shopping a bit later, then?"

"Don't be ridiculous." She frowned at him. Why were men so stupid? "And she buys the exact same things I do. Now she's getting on the same plane as me. It's freaking me out, Matt." Her hands had started to shake.

"Calm down, love. I'm sure it's just a coincidence."

"It's not! She's doing it on purpose. Why can't she just *fuck off* somewhere else?"

"Whoa, whoa, whoa! Rachel. Get a *grip*, sweetheart. She just shares your excellent taste, that's all."

"But look, Matt... look at what she's wearing... and her hand luggage!"

Matthew took in the woman's dark blue trouser suit and light blue wheelie case, then turned back to Rachel. She was wearing a dark blue trouser suit and beside her feet was a light blue wheelie case.

"Yeah, okay. That *is* a bit freaky," he agreed. "But she can't have copied you, can she? She had no idea what you would be wearing today. Let's be honest," he decided to add a joke to lighten the mood, "I've only just noticed myself, and I'm your husband!"

"So, let me get this straight, madam." The desk sergeant looked up from his notepad and met Rachel's eyes. "This woman has been following you around, copying your every move and you believe she is stalking you?"

Sardinia had been lovely. The beautiful blue Mediterranean, fabulous scenery, long walks with Matthew along secluded coastal paths. It should have been a holiday in paradise. But every morning, she was there at the breakfast buffet. Every evening, she was sitting in the dining room. An ominous presence, like a shadow Rachel couldn't shake off. She had ruined everything, and Rachel had resolved to make a complaint to Cambridge police first thing Monday morning.

"Yes, that's right sergeant. She's copied my every move over the past few weeks and I'm afraid she intends to do me harm. Why else would she be doing it?" She spread her palms and looked at him beseechingly.

"Well..." he looked up as the door to the interview room opened and another officer appeared. "Funnily enough, you are the second lady to make a similar complaint this morning. Seems we have a serial stalker on the loose."

Following the officer out of the interview room was a woman. A woman wearing a beige jacket over a white top and brown trousers... just like Rachel. A woman with a limp.

"*You!*" Rachel gasped. "You even followed me to the police station!"

"Erm... this lady was here first, Mrs Simpson," the desk sergeant pointed out. "She got here twenty minutes ago."

"And I've just filed a formal complaint about you," said the woman, imperiously, staring Rachel in the eye. "Imitating me, even following me on holiday. Some kind of psycho, if you ask me, Inspector," she said to the officer who'd accompanied her to the desk.

"A *psycho!* Well, you... you Gimpy Gertie!" spluttered Rachel in frustration.

"You're just a Copycat Kate!" spat the other woman.

The two policemen looked from one woman to the other. The Inspector spoke. "I think we might get to the bottom of this if you two ladies would join me in the interview room. Step this way, please."

"Right, then. Mrs Simpson... Mrs Maitland." The Inspector laid his hands on the table. "We've established that *neither* of you has deliberately tried to copy or imitate the other. You just *happen* to find yourselves in the same place at the same time, doing the same things, is that correct?"

"Yes, Yes," they both agreed.

"So neither of you is intentionally stalking the other and no crime has been committed. There must be some other reason for this... um... copycat behaviour."

They both nodded, reluctantly.

"This is not a matter for the police," he said, tidying up the papers before him. "You might like to seek advice or counselling elsewhere. But I'd suggest you have a good old chat between yourselves first, to find out what else you have in common." He raised his eyebrows to see how they responded to the idea. They looked at each other blankly.

"Have you considered the possibility that you two might be related?" he asked.

"Impossible! I don't have any brothers or sisters," said Rachel.

"I'm an only child," said Rebecca Maitland.

"Well," he said, "it's just a thought. But you *do* both *sound* very similar. Same hair, similar build. Are you a similar age, perhaps?"

"I was born on January 21st, 1981," said Rachel.

"Oh my God! So was I!" The two women stared at each other open-mouthed.

"Well... if I didn't know any better," said the Inspector, "I'd say you were sisters – twin sisters."

Over two identical cappuccinos in the Manikin Cafe, Rachel and Rebecca discovered they had both been adopted as infants. Rebecca had a particularly difficult childhood, filled with operations to repair life-threatening injuries caused in a fire. It was an accident that had scarred her for life and had so seriously affected her mother, she'd been told, that the poor woman had abandoned her and later took her own life.

Rachel reached across the table and held Rebecca's hand. She knew then, without a doubt. The woman she had unkindly referred to as Gimpy Gertie or Florence Nightmare, was, in fact, her identical twin sister. For the first time in thirty-seven years, Rachel and Rebecca could celebrate their similarities and rejoice in having something deeply, uncannily and blissfully in common.

CHAPTER 6

The Unmade Sea

I stumble from my unmade bed
To watch the unmade sea
Where mighty swells surge to the beach
And crash and churn, cold fingers reach
To claim the souls of wounded gulls
That limp among the broken hulls
Strewn by the surf-washed quay

Offshore the banshees rage and howl
To whip the spindrift's scream
The ocean's blankets toss and tumble
Sheets of foam criss-cross and crumple
Grey-green pillows topped with blue
Heap upon heap of wrack and spume
Poseidon's fevered dream

Beneath the churning, turbid waters
Below the roiling froth

Deep down where hungry shadows flit
Are silent screams when bodies bit
The crunch of shell and squelch of brains
Leave whispered hopes and scant remains
In silt and muddy broth

So as you drift in restful slumber
Spare a thought for those
Who lie beneath the ceaseless waves,
Know not the peace of earth-bound graves
But roll and rock in fitful sleep
Amid the nightmare of the deep
Their bones to decompose

And when along the sun-washed strand
A wreath of kelp you find
Remember then the maelstrom ferment
And spray and scud and tide and torment
From which the lords of chaos gripped
And tore that stem from rocks they ripped
With hidden lives entwined

CHAPTER 7

Repair Man

I didn't need this. I really, really didn't need this. From the approaching footsteps, it sounded as though I was going to get it anyway. Sure enough – tap, tap, tap on the bedroom door.

"It's eight o'clock, Rory!" Mother's voice. "You've got a job at nine, over in Oswestry."

A groan was all I could muster in reply.

"It doesn't do to get a reputation for lateness, Rory. You're not the only mobile mechanic in Shropshire..." She listened for an answer, but when none came, gave a heavy sigh. "There's fresh tea in the pot. Get up now, there's a good lad." The landing floorboards creaked as she made her way back towards the stairs.

*Good **lad**! I'm twenty-nine, for Christ's sake!*

I threw back the duvet and swung my legs out of bed, groaning again as I sat up and felt the full weight of my throbbing head. It was almost as bad as those stock exchange mornings after nights spent seeking refuge in drink and drugs. Those mornings that clubbed me in the brain when the alarm roused me for another day of gut-wrenching anguish. I didn't miss those.

Mum was on her way out of the kitchen door when I stumbled down the stairs. She looked back over her shoulder. "Tea's in the pot and there's porridge on the stove," she said.

I needed coffee and I hate porridge. "Thanks, Mum."

"I'm off to see to the sheep, so you'll have to sort yourself out now," she said, glancing at the kitchen clock. "You'll have to leave in ten minutes, mind, or you'll be late getting to Oswestry. And you've a call at twelve back here, Mrs Leverton, Barrett's Farm. Her Land Rover won't start. I've left you a note." She nodded at the bare wooden table where a mug, bowl and spoon awaited me. Propped between bowl and mug was a torn piece of paper with my day's jobs detailed.

"Thanks, Mum," I said again as the door clattered shut and the latch fell.

I poured the tea and searched the cupboard for painkillers. There was no justice in a head like this after I'd been dry and clean for seven months. Seven months since my father picked me up from Barts Hospital where I'd been pumped and de-toxed for the last time. That's what the consultant said. There'd be no next time. Another session would be my last. My dad had said nothing on the drive back to the farm, but his silence spoke volumes.

I took two tablets with a gulp of the hot brown liquid and felt my stomach protest. A glance in the breadbin told me I'd be eating porridge or nothing. I forced down a bowl of warm gloop before stepping into the grey dawn in search of Dad's ancient Morris van. By the time the old rust-bucket had creaked and wheezed its way to Oswestry, my head had cleared just enough to cope with the diesel fumes and pig slurry that came with my first job of the day.

I'd always found the stench of farms revolting. It was one of the reasons I'd persevered at college. Anything to get away from the stink, the drudgery and the poverty of my parents' farm. The bright lights of London and the excitement of the stock exchange had seemed like paradise. At first.

Old man Hackett showed me where to find his broken-down tractor – abandoned in a rainbow-streaked pool of mud and diesel where it had croaked its last – and left me to it.

"It's buggered," was all the information he shared before returning to his grunting, squealing, reeking stockyard.

Two hours of skinned knuckles and curses, plus some imaginative use of wire and gaffer tape, fixed the leaking pump, repaired a burst hose and replaced the heater plug. Ted Hackett grudgingly paid me fifty quid in crumpled ten-pound notes and laughed at my suggestion that the old Ferguson would benefit from a service. It was par for the course in Shropshire's farming community.

After a quick clean up at his outside tap, I was back in the Morris, sowing a trail of blue smoke to Barrett's Farm, five miles south of my parents' place. The whole district had revelled in gossip last autumn when Ralph Leverton ran off with the Latvian girl who'd come to help with the harvest. I was grateful at the time, as it diverted attention from the drug-and-drink addled prodigal son who had returned from spectacular failure in London.

There was another olfactory assault as I passed the stench of the sewage works and turned up the rutted and pot-holed track to Barrett's Farm.

It was a stark contrast to evenings spent with fragrant young women in the city's financial district, when Chanel and Dior would lift my spirits and fire my passion. It was all a distant memory now that I'd sunk to the bottom of the dung heap once again.

Even my last few investments, stupidly locked into high-risk term options, looked set to disappear down the toilet within days, judging by the financial reviews I was reading. I'd spent hours on my laptop last night, desperately trying to extricate the last of my cash, before conceding defeat in the early hours of the morning. I'd collapsed into bed with an aching head, knowing that my mother was right. I needed to get my eyes tested, but figured I wasn't old enough for glasses. Staring at screens had damaged my sight, just as surely as the stock exchange had ruined my health and self-esteem.

Even so, I didn't envy June Leverton's lot, trying to run Barrett's Farm on her own. The modest farmhouse and outbuildings needed maintenance, and the old Land Rover that I'd come to fix stood forlorn outside, slab-sided in faded olive green.

"Hello! You must be Rory?" She came out to greet me with a smile, tucking a strand of hair behind her ear. Her dirty dungarees couldn't hide a pleasantly curvy figure. The Latvian girl must have been something special, I thought, for her husband to run off and leave such a good-looking woman behind.

"Not beyond hope... is it?" she asked. I was about to pay her a compliment when I realised she was referring to the Land Rover.

"Oh, no. These old girls keep going forever," I said, and immediately felt stupid. Did she think I was calling her an 'old girl'? "I'll g-get my tools," I stammered and pulled open the back doors to the van, one of which sagged dangerously on its hinges, producing a shower of rust.

"It's been getting harder to start," she explained, "but yesterday morning there was nothing... and I think I've flattened the battery now."

"No problem, Mrs Leverton. I'll take a look at it for you."

"Please, call me June," she said. "Would you like a cup of tea?"

"Ah..." I looked at her hopefully. "I could murder a cup of coffee, Mrs Lev... June. But can I wait until I'm finished? Never tastes right when I'm covered in diesel." I smiled and raised my hands as if to prove it.

"Of course!" she said. "I'll put the kettle on."

An hour later and the old Land Rover coughed and spluttered into life. After filling the yard with thick black smoke for a minute or two, it was now purring contentedly.

"I'll leave it to run," I said over the rumbling exhaust note, as I stepped into the kitchen to wash my hands. "It'll purge the last of the water out of the fuel system and put a bit more charge into the battery."

"Fine," she said, closing the door to keep out the noise and smoke. "I'm so pleased you could get it going. How much do I owe you?" Her eyebrows rose enticingly.

"Oh... including the filter, it'll be thirty pounds, please."

"That's very reasonable. Look... I hope this won't sound too... um... strange, coming from an older woman." June Leverton reached up and unhooked one side of her dungarees' bib, revealing a well-filled pink T-shirt. "But is there any way we could negotiate on the price, Rory? Things have been a bit tight, financially, since my husband left..."

"Well... um..." I was about to say my prices were already rock bottom, when she unhooked the other side of her bib and looked me straight in the eye.

"What did you have in mind?" I asked, stupidly.

"Could I trade..." she said, taking a step towards me, "an hour in bed for your hour of mechanical expertise...?" I looked up from her T-shirt to find a seductive smile.

"Sure, but... I smell of diesel... and farms." I held my hands out apologetically.

"Oh, we all smell of farms, Rory," she said taking another step and grasping my hand. "Besides," she added with a wink, "I *need* it. Don't you?"

For the first time since I'd left London in disgrace, I drove back to my parents' farm with a smile on my face. Okay, so I was thirty quid down on the morning, but I felt immeasurably richer. Compared to the fragrant and flouncy girls I'd known in London, Mrs Leverton – sorry – June, was warm, willing and wonderful. My one regret was that I'd got her Land Rover going in only an hour. I'd like to have kept *her* going for the whole afternoon.

After the coffee she'd promised earlier, and some chit-chat about what I'd been doing with myself in London, she'd said goodbye with a peck on the cheek. "Nice doing business with you, Rory." She had a twinkle in her eye. "I'll call you if anything else needs fixing."

"Ah... um... it's my mother who takes the calls, so..." I mumbled.

"Don't worry. I'll be discreet." She waved as I set off down the rutted and pot-holed track.

And she was. A week later I changed a wheel bearing on her tractor and provided a full service in her bedroom. "You know, Rory," she said over coffee afterwards, "there are lots of little jobs need doing around here. To save me phoning your mum every week, how about I book you for Monday afternoons until further notice...?"

The arrangement suited me fine. I was out of the dating scene on account of being on the wagon and permanently broke. June got her farm machinery fixed and we both fulfilled a need without any money changing hands and no strings attached. Or so we thought.

As spring turned into summer and my weekly visits to Barrett's Farm became a regular fixture, both June and I grew more relaxed in each other's company and, dare I say it, we became very good friends. The fact that she was ten years older than me didn't seem to matter. By late summer we were more than lovers and my visits were more than weekly. I was actively looking for jobs around Barrett's Farm, not because I needed an excuse for more time in bed, but because I cared about June's welfare. We never said the words, but we both knew we'd fallen in love.

That was when I took it upon myself to fix the hay baler. June had told me it had swallowed a rock last autumn and was permanently out of action. Beyond repair, she'd said, which was why it was buried under sacks and boxes at the back of the barn. But with the hay nearly ready for harvesting, I decided I ought to find out what was wrong with it, or she'd have no stock feed for the winter. While she was on the quad bike rounding up the sheep one Monday afternoon, I pulled the baler away from the barn wall and crawled inside the main chute to suss out what was broken.

It was battered, alright, but it didn't look like a rock had been through it. Snagged on a bolt head deep inside, I found a scrap of material with a button attached. Puzzled, I crawled back out to look at it in the daylight. It had a floral pattern and looked like it might have come from a girl's summer dress. An awful image began to form in my mind.

"I *thought* I told you not to work on the baler, Rory." June was standing at the barn door. She sounded more sad than angry. "We had a good thing going, you and me. Now you've gone and ruined everything." With that she turned and walked away. I found her sitting at her kitchen table, crying.

"It was an accident. A complete accident, I swear it," she said, through the sobs.

I was too shocked to say anything, so I sat and listened.

"I knew *something* was going on," she said, sniffing into a screwed-up tissue. "Ralph was quite taken with Marta, the Latvian girl. But I thought it was just flirting, you know... older man getting the hots for a pretty young thing. I didn't imagine for a moment that they might actually be doing it, right under my nose.

"I was looking after the sheep, like I usually do. Ralph was teaching Marta how to operate the tractor and baler, harvesting the hay down in the south pasture. It's out of sight from most of the farm, but I could hear the tractor and thought they were just getting on with the baling. It was a hot afternoon, and I thought I'd take them a drink.

When I got there the tractor was chugging away but not moving.

"I walked all around and called out Ralph's name. I guess he couldn't hear me over the noise of the engine. I put two and two together and decided they must have gone down to the spinney. There was only one reason they'd do that. I was angry, of course, but mostly surprised they'd gone off with the job half done, leaving the tractor running. Sounds stupid now, but I remember thinking, 'they might at least have finished the baling before they skived off for a bonk in the spinney'.

"I decided *I'd* finish the baling – there were only two more rows to do – and then, when they came back from the spinney, they'd know they'd been caught out. I jumped up on the tractor, jammed it in gear and set off down the row of hay. I didn't imagine for one moment they would be *in* the hay itself. With that old baler you drive beside the row, so you don't see what the baler is gathering in."

June turned to me with wide, wet eyes. "Honest to God, Rory. I had no idea they were in there. No idea at all. Then there was this great bang and clatter. By the time I'd stopped the tractor it was too late. There was blood everywhere and a bale with arms hanging out the side. You've never seen anything so hideous in your life. I checked their pulses, but they were both dead.

"I sat there in the field in total shock, wondering what the hell to do. It was such an absurd accident... I could see how the police would assume I'd caught them at it and done them both in deliberately. Even if it was classed as manslaughter, I'd get put away for years. I was scared witless, Rory. In a complete panic. Not thinking straight at all."

June shook her head slowly at the memory. "So I did a stupid thing. I decided to hide their bodies and say they'd run away together. It happens all the time. Older man, younger woman... they run off and make a new life for themselves. I couldn't bring them back, so I invented a new life for them. They were living incognito somewhere, having a fine old time. I almost began to believe it myself after a while."

I finally found my voice. "So... erm... what did you do with their bodies?"

"Made a stack of bales at the end of the field, right next to the sewage works. They're right at the bottom. The smell of sewage is overpowering down there, so I thought—"

"Fucking hell, June! You've buried your *hus-*

band and a Latvian girl under a haystack – beside a sewage works! How *could* you?"

She buried her face in her hands and groaned. "I know you think I'm a monster. But I was scared. I didn't know what else to do."

"You should have gone straight to the police. Told them exactly what happened. If they'd found the bodies in a bale at the back of the machine, they'd have *seen* it was an accident."

"I know. I know. I've gone over this a thousand times—"

"Now you've had the bodies hidden for a year, what're they going to think...?"

She lifted her face and stared at me with wide, sad eyes.

"You *have* to tell them, June! You can't go on living with this... this... *nightmare* hanging over your head. The bodies are going to be discovered *sometime*, aren't they...?"

She lowered her eyes and nodded slowly. "After all this time I'd started to believe maybe they wouldn't be found. Then this nice repair man came along and made me feel almost human again. I kidded myself that maybe I *could* have a life, after all..."

Despite the horror of her revelation, I felt a wave of sorrow for her. I reached across the table and squeezed her hand. “You *have* to tell them, June. You can’t go on living a lie.”

“You tell them,” she said quietly.

“What!?”

“You tell them, Rory. Please...?” She looked me in the eye. “I can’t face going into the police station and explaining it all. You tell them... would you do that for me?”

I pushed my chair back and stood up. My head was spinning.

“Yes,” she said. “Go now. Right away, Rory. Let’s get this over and done with.”

I ran outside, fired up the old Morris van and set off down the rutted, pot-holed track. Turned left on to the main road and slowed as I approached the sewage works. There was the haystack. I stopped the van. Great round bales, piled one on top of the other, gone grey from a year’s weather. Hiding their gruesome secret.

“Nobody leaves a stack of hay to rot like that,” I muttered to myself. “Too valuable when you’ve got animals to feed.” A thought struck me.

I swung the van round in the road, getting a blaring horn from a passing car. I turned back up the track to Barrett’s Farm, bumping and lurching from pot hole to pot hole. I couldn’t let her go to prison because of an *accident*. It was her stupid husband's fault, not hers. I loved her, whatever she'd done. And I had an idea that could hide the evidence forever.

As the van rattled and banged its way back to the farmhouse, another thought struck me. Why had she sent me off to the police station? All she had to do was pick up the phone – or get me to phone for her. A police car would be here within minutes. A cold bead of sweat trickled down my spine as I pulled up outside the door with a screech of tyres. As the van door swung open I heard a thunderous boom from kitchen.

"JUNE! NO!" I screamed and ran inside. She was slumped over the kitchen table, shotgun on the floor beside her. "NO! No, nononononono," I whimpered as I threw my arms around her torso.

"I couldn't do it," she muttered.

"OH, thank GOD!"

"Too much of a coward. Couldn't even put an end to it all."

"June, look at me!" I pulled her upright and held her shoulders. "We *don't* have to tell the police. I've got an idea. Nobody will find them, trust me."

She looked at me dazed and confused.

"I'm not letting anyone put you in prison. We'll sort this out together, okay?"

"But... I can't let you get involved, Rory. You'll be as guilty as me."

"I already *am* involved. I love you, June. And we've both got things in our past that are best left buried."

"Oh, Rory... my sweet Repair Man." She smiled through her tears and pulled me into a hug.

"I love you too," she whispered in my ear. "I need repairing every day. Move in with me. Please?"

"I thought you'd never ask," I said with a grin. "Now put that bloody gun away before we have any more accidents. I'll pop back home, tell my mum I'm going to be living here and bring a few things, although I haven't got much. And tonight we'll set about hiding the evidence for good."

CHAPTER 8

Dear Mom

Dear Mom,

Thought I'd write you a few lines while I'm waiting for my train. Yes, I'm heading south again. At least it'll be warmer than Chicago. Aunt Kimiko has been very good to me these past few days and sends you her love. I know you wanted me home for the holidays, but I couldn't face your pitying looks. Or the questions from my little sister. There's nothing I could tell her that would make any sense. Just make sure she finishes school and gets a decent job, something that will make you proud.

I didn't have that choice. After all those years of internment, just because of our name, I had no grades and no prospects. Nobody is hiring us. Not for regular work. One look at my hair or my eyes and it's 'no vacancy', every time. I know you do the best you can with your sewing, but ever since Dad died at the Tule Lake camp, we were never going to make ends meet when they let us out, were we, Mom? And that no-good boyfriend of mine took to drinking and poker once he got me down south. He broke my heart and left me with nowhere else to go.

I hope you are looking forward to 1950. Every year puts that awful war a little further behind us. One day we will be seen as honest citizens again and people will no longer shun us in the street. Ironically, it is my looks that got me this job. Well, job is too fine a word. Profession, I suppose. Orientals, they call us. It's better than Japs or Nips. But it pays well, and I will keep sending the checks home so you can keep a roof over your head, and Hayami can finish her schooling. Whatever you do, Mom, make sure she doesn't follow me into this. It's no life for a young girl. In truth, it's no life at all.

Well, the train is at the platform, so I'll finish now and drop this in the mailbox. Give Hayami a big hug and a kiss for me and try not to despise me for this awful choice I've made.

Your loving daughter
Madoka

PS If you want to write me, you can send a letter to West 34th Street, New Orleans,
You know the name of the place, don't you? The House of the Rising Sun.

The House of the Rising Sun is a traditional folk song said to have been known by miners in 1905. The earliest published version of the lyrics dates from 1925.

I chose this song for a writing challenge because of its raw, emotional edge, and set about researching an alternative idea for what might lie behind the title. What I discovered was a sad chapter in history concerning the plight of Japanese Americans during the Second World War.

Between 110,000 - 120,000 people of Japanese ancestry, most of them second or third generation American citizens living on the Pacific coast, were removed from their homes and incarcerated in concentration camps in the western interior of the country. Nine of the ten camps were shut down by the end of 1945, but Tule Lake, which held prisoners slated for deportation to Japan, was not closed until March 20, 1946, over 4 years after the internment began.

On release, most found they had lost their homes and farms and could not find employment due to their Japanese heritage. Thirty-four years later, in 1980, Congress established the Commission on Wartime Relocation and Internment of Civilians. In 1983 it issued a report entitled Personal Justice Denied, condemning the internment as unjust and motivated by racism and xenophobia rather than military necessity. In 1988 financial redress was approved and by 1998, $1.6 billion had been paid to the camps' survivors. 81,800 people qualified for payment.

There have been many recordings of The House of the Rising Sun by different artists, but perhaps the most haunting rendition – the one that inspired my 'Dear Mom' letter from Madoka – was recorded by Bob Dylan in 1962.

I recommend you listen to his studio version of this moving song. You can find it on YouTube here - https://www.youtube.com/watch?v=ZdXssUp7cOk

CHAPTER 9

Twitch

Conditions were perfect. The jet-black sky, sprinkled with stars, was beginning to lighten in the east. Ducks were starting their morning squabbles out on the lagoon and the geese would be arriving soon. Derek shivered and reached for his Thermos flask. He loved this time of day and the solitude of the reserve. It was well worth the early start and freezing bike ride. From his favourite spot in the seaward hide he often saw glimpses of rare birds, water voles and otters that late-comers missed.

He blew at the steam rising from the rim of his plastic cup and sipped the hot tea his mum had made, keeping his eyes trained on the dark patch of reeds across the water. You never knew when you might see a...

"What was *that!*" he muttered to himself, reaching for his binoculars. Orange flashes among the foliage were certainly unusual. He quickly discounted fireflies. Wrong colour and wrong time of year. Besides, these had been three regular flashes. He searched his memory bank for identification and realised they could be only one thing – a vehicle. *Yes,* he smiled to himself. *Easy one – a car's hazard lights giving three quick blinks when the doors were locked.*

Derek lowered his binoculars, or bins as he called them, and turned his attention back to the reeds that were just beginning to show in the first glimmer of early morning light. He might spot little grebes surfacing amongst them soon. But he found he couldn't concentrate. The orange flashes had unsettled him.

It wasn't that there shouldn't be a vehicle out there – he knew there was an industrial estate on the far side of the reserve – it was simply the wrong time of day. He checked his watch, the chunky adventurer's watch his dad had given him for Christmas, and saw it was still only 5.22. He'd seen activity on the estate often enough, lorries coming and going, but only during the daytime. Nobody would be working *this* early in the morning... surely? He reached for his bins again.

The trouble was, it was still so dark over

there, he couldn't make out anything through the reeds and bushes that filled the horizon. He couldn't see any buildings, let alone cars or people. He sighed and was about to resume his personal nature study on the lagoon, when a small rectangle of dim light appeared briefly. A dark shape appeared in it, but before he could focus the bins the light had gone again. *Easy one – door opening in building, person passing through.*

At least he now knew where to look. He put down his bins and reached for his telescope. It was too heavy and cumbersome for normal use in the hide – he brought it for field work on his long walks around the reserve's perimeter – but its extra power might help with this impromptu spying mission.

Derek got the 'scope trained in the right direction and was fiddling with the focus when the rectangle of light appeared again, bigger and brighter this time. Immediately he saw one – he counted – two, three people emerge before the door closed and the light disappeared. To the left came three bright orange flashes. He panned and focussed in time to see a car door opening, revealing a dim interior light. Two people got in and the door closed. Then another door opened – the driver's door? – and the third, larger, person got in. The interior light faded as the car moved off, but without any head-lamps or rear lights showing. "Oh, yeah!" he muttered. "So... you don't want to be seen, do you? I wonder what you're up to?"

Derek felt a thrill tingle his spine. His clandestine surveillance had spotted some distinctly dodgy activity going on over on the Felixstowe East Industrial Estate. He celebrated with a swig of tea and heard the first distant honk of the approaching geese. Maybe this was the morning he'd spot a garganey, the rare striped duck he'd been waiting for on its migration from the south. He smiled and picked up his bins again. This was turning into a first-class birding morning.

"Hello, love." Derek's mum looked up from the cooker as he stepped through the kitchen door. "You look pleased with yourself. Did you see some good birds this morning?"

"Yeah. G-g-garganeys. F-first of the year." He smiled at her and dropped his camouflaged rucksack on the floor. He peeled off the high-vis waistcoat she insisted he wore when riding his bike, and shrugged off his bulky camouflaged jacket. He'd decided on the ride home that he wouldn't mention the dodgy goings-on he'd also witnessed on the industrial estate. His mum worried about him enough as it was, without thinking he was spying on some illegal activity while he was out.

"*Oh*... take your stuff to your room, please, Derek... and *wipe* your boots before you go. I don't want you spreading bird poo throughout the house."

He cleaned his boots carefully on the coconut mat by the kitchen door, then picked up his bag and shuffled sideways past the kitchen table.

"And don't be too long in the bathroom," she called after him. "Your breakfast is in the pan now, so it'll be ready to eat in five minutes."

"Mmm, n-n-nice breakfast, Mum, thanks." Derek lifted his fork to deliver another piece of bacon and egg to his mouth.

"Oh... try to take *care*, Derek. It's going everywhere!" His mother's brow furrowed. She shook her head in resignation.

"D-d-doing my best, Mum," he said, as his hand jerked wildly and another fine spray of egg yolk splattered the tablecloth.

"Oh, *dear!*" she said as she reached for the dishcloth.

"L-leave it, Mum. I'll c-clean it up after."

At twenty-seven, Derek's tics and stammer were not going to get any better. He'd been through every type of treatment the health service could offer since childhood and they'd finally concluded it was just one of those things. He was stuck with it for life. He'd tried to get a job, but it had proved hopeless. Nobody wanted to employ a gangly man who couldn't talk properly and shook like a leaf whenever he had to hold anything. Especially when he had to hold something important or fragile.

It was only when he was birding that Derek's hands behaved themselves. When he wanted to focus his bins or 'scope on some rare species, a calm descended upon him and all the shaking ceased. Unless, that was, some other bird-spotter spoke to him and Derek tried to answer without stammering. Then his hands would start to shake, and he'd have to gather up his things and move on.

It was a funny thing, he thought. He had been nicknamed 'Twitch' at school and tormented over his stammer throughout his childhood. But it was only when he was actually *twitching*– birding on his own – that his tics stopped. He'd always enjoyed the peace and serenity of the countryside. The discovery that it was the perfect therapy for his frustrating condition came as a delightful bonus.

After finishing his breakfast and giving the kitchen table and nearby wall a rudimentary wipe down, Derek thanked his mum with a smeary kiss on her forehead and retired to his room. There he fired up his old laptop and logged on to his Facebook account. The internet birding groups he belonged to provided a camaraderie and anonymity that suited him perfectly. His profile, named The Wicked Twitch, showed a photo of him in full camo gear, with hood up and bins in front of his eyes. Only his manic grin gave a hint at the personality beneath.

One group in particular, East Coast Birders, received much of his attention as he was one of its founders and an admin for the page. As always, his Norfolk Broads-based pal, Once Bittern, had sent him a string of crude and cryptic messages.

<you outa bed yet you lazy
git? Its clear over Barton.
Grebes doing courtship
dance – randy bgrs>

<hope you getting summat
down your way?>

<you outa bed yet Twitch?>

Derek smiled. He always had a good banter with Bittern. Theirs was a friendly rivalry, urging each other on with sighting comparisons and inappropriate jokes. He was the only online friend who knew of Derek's tics and stammering. They'd confided in each other one particularly wet and dismal day, when even the hardiest birder saw the sense in staying home for R&R, or Research & Recognition, as they called it. Bittern told him he'd got into birding to hide his horrendous teenage acne and the scarring it had left him with. The birds didn't seem to notice, he'd said. After that, they'd called each other Twitch and Bitch, for no good reason except it made them smile.

Derek typed a reply

<I was up at 4, Bitch, in
the hide at 5, while you
were still snoring.
And the garganey have
arrived>
<Twitch1, Bitch 0>
<Also caught crims doing

dodgy deals on industrial estate beyond reserve>

<Photos – or it didn't happen>

<I'll take phone tomoz. And my NV kit. See if I can snap them in the act>

<No shit, Sherlock!>

Derek was proud of his birding kit, most of which had been bought for him by his parents as birthday and Christmas gifts. He'd bought the NV, or night vision, lens himself from his meagre savings. It made a huge difference in low light conditions and he'd caught some great images of owls and other creatures of the night in the year since he first tried it out. Derek logged off the internet and laid out his birding equipment on his bed. He'd make sure it was cleaned and his phone fully charged before he went to bed. It would be another early night ready for a 4am alarm call tomorrow.

The gravel path crunched, and his bike's tyres skittered as Derek pedalled along the reserve's perimeter track towards the seaward hide. It was a good job he knew it well as he'd turned his lights off when he left the main road and was navigating by moonlight alone. No point in alerting the crims there was someone about to set up surveillance from the reserve, was there? If they were crims, that is. And if they were still there, of course.

He arrived at the hide and leaned his bike against its wooden wall. The familiar smell of pine and preservative hit him as he opened the door. *Good – nobody here.* There were occasions when other birders turned up early, like a particularly high tide that drove waders from the estuary, but not today. Derek took up his favourite position at the far end, unloading his rucksack and laying out his kit in the darkness. A scuffling noise made him reach up to his head torch, clicking it on in time to see a rat scuttling out of the door. He didn't mind rats, they were all part of nature, but he didn't particularly want to share the hide with one. Especially while he was trying to concentrate on activity on the industrial estate, which was mostly hidden by reeds and trees, even when it was daylight.

Derek was reaching for his flask to pour a warming cuppa, when he saw distant orange flashes. He brought up his bins in time to see the faint rectangle of light open and close. *Bit earlier today, then?*

He checked his watch. 5.03. So, they were still there, but what were they doing? Time to take up his new spying position, an idea he'd dreamt up just as he was falling asleep last night. He hung his bins round his neck, unscrewed the tripod from his 'scope and fitted the night vision lens. Then he hung that round his neck as well and walked across the creaky plank floorboards to the hut door.

Outside he repositioned his bike against the wall of the hide to make sure it wouldn't fall over, then climbed on to the crossbar as the bike wobbled and shook beneath him. With his shoulders above the sloping roof of the hide, Derek lifted his right leg until his knee rested on the top. Then, after a deep breath, he pulled the rest of his body up on to the roof. He was congratulating himself on his successful climb when he heard the clatter of his bike falling over and realised getting down would not be quite so easy. Oh well, he'd cross that bridge later.

Derek crawled on hands and knees to the upper edge of the sloping roof and lay prone, peering out over the dark marshes. At times like this, he liked to imagine himself as a sniper, lining up his next target, but as he brought his bins up he saw he was too late. His target was leaving. The car drove off, its interior light fading, from the back of the warehouse. With no lights showing at all it was difficult to see, but Derek could just make out its black shape moving along the side of the ugly square building. The car's brake lights flashed briefly before it turned on to the estate's service road and disappeared.

"Dammit!" he muttered under his breath. "Too late."

He lowered the bins and brought the 'scope up to his eye. It was even more unwieldy with the night vision lens attached, but he finally got it pointing the right way and turned the focus ring. Even with only a sliver of Moon, there was enough light for the NV lens to show up the warehouse clearly... and halfway along its back wall was a slim triangle of light. Derek brought it into sharp focus and realised immediately what it was. *Easy one – gap in a curtain.* It must be a poorly-lit room, he decided, with something like sacking draped as an ineffective blackout.

He studied the dim rectangle of window with the bright gap in its corner for a minute and saw a light flare and flicker for a second before going out. *Easy one – someone lighting a cigarette.* He imagined a gang of bank robbers standing around a blackboard chalked with the diagram of their next raid, and his pulse quickened. Derek reached into his jacket pocket for his mobile phone, turned it on and clicked it into the mount on the scope's eyepiece.

In truth, he had no idea what was going on inside the warehouse. It might be entirely innocent. But he would capture a few images and send them to Bittern with some tantalising descriptions. Derek smiled. That should get the banter flying nicely.

With a few photos of the window in the bag, including one showing another cigarette being lit (chain smoking was a sure sign of a criminal mind, he thought), Derek was ready to upload them to Bittern's facebook messages. He took a wide angle shot with the phone alone for context – dark and blurry, but it showed the outline of the warehouse okay – and started sending them across. To his surprise, his birding pal replied immediately.

<Think you've lost it, Twitch.
It's a night watchman having
a fag at the end of his shift,
feet up inside his warehouse>
<Hardly 'criminal activity'
is it?>

<There was a car with no
lights again, but I missed
it>

<Stop tossing around and

get some pix of those garganeys.
Unless you imagined them too?>

Derek sighed and turned the scope towards the lagoon. There was lots of activity, ducks squabbling over mating rights and geese cruising past with their heads held high, appearing contemptuous of their smaller, bickering cousins. But even with the NV lens he couldn't make out any stripy garganeys. After an extended inspection of the lagoon and surrounding reed beds, Derek decided it was time to get down from the roof and have a cup of tea. His elbows were aching and there was no telling how much bird poo he was lying in up here. His mum would have something to say about that.

As he clipped the lens cap back on his scope, Derek noticed a brief red flash from the industrial estate, then another followed by a continuous white light. He removed the lens cap and brought the scope back up. Maybe the car had returned? *No! Better than that! It's a lorry, reversing...*

Derek scrambled to fish his phone out of his jacket pocket and clipped it on. He took a series of pics of the artic reversing down the side of the warehouse. They were as clear as day with his NV kit. Then the brake lights came back on as the vehicle stopped and all its lights went out. Two men appeared at the rear and unlocked the back doors to the trailer. Derek fumbled with his phone to select video and set it running as the doors swung open and people started to climb out.

Cripes! That's an easy one – people trafficking! Bittern won't sneer at this...

They were all women. Even from this distance, the power of his telescope showed them clearly, some wearing jeans, a couple in headscarves, all carrying rucksacks. He counted nine of them, walking in single file, following one of the men around the back of the warehouse. Light flooded out as the warehouse door opened, the women filed through it followed by the man, then the door shut.

Derek panned back to the lorry, where the second man was locking the trailer doors before disappearing behind its far side. A few moments later the brake lights flashed briefly before the lorry started to move forward, back to the estate road, where it turned right and moved out of sight. Back at the rear of the warehouse, there was a glow behind the sack curtain as another cigarette was lit. Then nothing. Derek stopped recording and brought up his message page to Bittern.

<How's this then, Bitch?
Lorry just arrived and
unloaded 9 women>

Derek uploaded his video file and waited with a satisfied smile. He didn't have to wait long.

<Bloody hell, Twitch!
That's more like it. Illegal
immigrants, ain't they?
You got people smugglers
caught in the act, mate!>

<What now? Phone
the police?>

<Hold on a mo.
Watching it again>

Derek checked the length of video. The whole thing had lasted only 1 minute 13 seconds. Sure enough, Bittern was messaging again.

<Pity we can't see the
reg on the lorry or the
police could pick him
up too>

<So, what do you think? Call
the cops?>

<You said there was a car

came yesty>

<Yeah, took two of them
away>

<This is a holding pen, Twitch.
Keeping them outa sight until
they can move em on>

<What do you think they're
doing with them?>

<Sex trade, most likely.
Shipping em off to brothels
all over the country, I reckon>

Derek thought of the TV news and the desperate refugees from Syria, Afghanistan and Sudan. These poor women had escaped one hell only to be sold into another. He was about to send Bittern another message when he saw movement next to the warehouse. He set the phone to video and brought the scope up again.

It was a white van, a longish panel van that had seen better days. It drove around the back of the warehouse and parked in front of the door and window. A man climbed out of the driver's seat and walked around the back of the vehicle. After he'd vanished, Derek assumed he had entered the warehouse too. He trained the scope on the van's number plate and fiddled with the focus, trying to read the registration, but it was impossible. He uploaded the second video clip to Bittern.

<Another vehicle just arrived. Can't quite make out registration though>

<Can you get any closer, Twitch?>

<Yeah. If I walk around the reserve track, I can get a lot closer>

<Sup to you, mate. Call the cops now, or try to get a decent pic of the van's reg>

<I'll try to get the reg before van goes>

<Okay. Take care mate. Keep me posted>

Derek held the scope and bins against his chest as he shuffled down the slope of the roof. There was enough light for him to see his bicycle lying on its side on the ground below. He moved along the roof to avoid landing on it and after a moment's hesitation, launched himself off the edge. It wasn't far down to the gravel track, and Derek managed to land without damaging his optical gear or himself.

He ran in to the hide, grabbed his rucksack and stuffed his thermos inside before jamming his arms through the straps. Back outside, he picked his bike up, climbed on board and set off pedalling for the far side of the reserve, hoping he would get there before the white van drove off again.

Ten sweaty minutes later he was within fifty yards of the main road and as close to the back of the warehouse as he could get. Derek jumped off his bike and leant it against a bush. It was now almost full daylight and the sun would be coming up over the sea any minute, so he hid behind the bush while he sorted his kit out. A brief look through the bins showed the van's registration plate was visible, but not readable. The scope with its NV lens would pick it up, no problem.

Derek clipped his phone to the scope's eyepiece and set it to video. He brought the scope up and trained it on the van. A bit of juggling with focus and the van's registration numbers and letters showed up clearly. *Gottit!* He uploaded the video file to Bittern.

<There you go, Bitch. Van's
reg, clear as day>

<Nice one. Now, if I was you,
I'd cycle off somewhere safe
and call the cops.>

<Hold on. Van's on the
move again>

Derek brought the scope up in time to see the van reverse and then set off at speed. He panned back to the rear of the warehouse where he noticed an upper window. And in it was a man, staring at him through a pair of binoculars.

Oh, shit!

Derek stuffed his phone in his pocket, let the scope hang from its strap around his neck, grabbed his bike and swung his leg over the seat. He set off pedalling hard down the track, cursing under his breath. Just as he got to the road, the white van pulled across the end of the track, knocking his front wheel from beneath him. He bounced off the passenger door and hit the ground, where he lay, stunned and winded.

"Bit careless, that, ridin' into the main road without lookin'." A man with a tattoo on his cheek was reaching down. Derek raised his arm, expecting a hand up, but the man grabbed his telescope instead. "'Specially when yer carryin' fancy spyin' gear."

"N-n-no! B-b-bird watching." Derek grabbed the strap to stop the man pulling it over his head.

"Suit yerself." The man calmly knelt on Derek's chest, making him gasp, and used a knife to slice through the strap.

"P-p-please!" Derek reached for it in vain, his hand twitching with anxiety.

Tattoo Man held the vicious-looking sheath knife in front of Derek's face. "Yer a right spazzer, aren't yer? Put yer 'and down and keep still." He studied the telescope and frowned at the empty clamp fitted to the eye-piece.

"Okay, so where's yer camera, bird boy?"

"N-n-no camera." Derek heard a door slam and boots advancing on the road.

"Yer phone then." Tattoo Man pressed the knife against Derek's cheek. "Come on, 'and it over."

Another face appeared, unshaven and angry, with slick greasy hair and a ponytail at the back. "What take so long?" he grunted in a deep Eastern European accent.

"Spazzy bird boy 'ere can't remember where 'e put 'is phone."

"Then keel him."

"NO! F-f-f-fone!" Derek scrabbled in his jacket

pocket and produced the phone. Tattoo Man took it, then grasped the front of Derek's jacket and hauled him to his feet. The man with the pony-tail picked up his bike, spun around and threw it effortlessly out into the lagoon. It sank out of sight, leaving only a few bubbles at the surface. Derek was dragged to the van and shoved in through the passenger door. Tattoo Man slid in behind him as Pony-tail got in the driver's door, trapping Derek between them.

With a roar from the engine, a squeal from the tyres and graunching from the gearbox, the van was reversed, turned and hurried back towards the industrial estate. Within seconds they pulled up at the rear the warehouse where Derek was dragged out of the van and pushed in through the door. Inside, sitting in a row on the floor with their backs against the wall, were the nine women. They all turned scared, exhausted eyes towards him as he was shoved towards a metal staircase at the far end.

"Up!" said Tattoo Man, giving Derek a prod in the kidneys. Their feet rang on the steel rungs as they climbed to a door and into a small room. Sitting in a plastic chair behind a battered table, was a swarthy, middle-aged man in a shiny charcoal-grey suit.

"So, this is snoopin' bastard?" he said in a thick accent, similar to Ponytail.

"J-just b-b-bird watchin'," stammered Derek.

"We'll see," he said, reaching out for the phone that Tattoo Man handed to him. He pressed a switch, frowned, and said: "How you open it?"

Derek was pushed forwards. With his hands twitching violently, it took him three goes to draw the shape on the phone's screen that unlocked it. The man rapidly flicked through the list of apps and opened the call register. "You call someone?" He grunted the question.

"N-no."

"Send message?" He opened the SMS folder.

"N-nobody."

"Email?"

Derek shook his head. Silently he prayed the man wouldn't open his Facebook account.

"Okay, let's see what pictures you take..." He tapped the gallery icon, and sucked in a noisy breath. "So... video of van... and lorry bring girls." He looked up at Derek. "You work for police?"

"N-n-no!" Derek saw his hands shaking uncontrollably. "J-just b-b-bird watching. That's all. You k-k-keep the phone. Let me go... I w-w-won't tell anybody."

"Ha! Don' think so. You know wha' happen to curious cat, don' you?" He lay Derek's phone on the table, drew a pistol from inside his jacket and brought the butt of the handle crashing down on the screen. He gestured towards the door with his chin. "Teck him down. Send up Dmytro."

Derek was pushed back down the steel steps and made to sit on the floor facing the women.

"Danylo wants you," said Tattoo Man to Ponytail, who had been slouching against the wall. He ran up the steel staircase and slammed the office door shut behind him. Tattoo Man took up his position near the outside door. Escape, Derek realised, would be impossible. He leaned his head back against the wall and tried to stop his hands from shaking.

"You look scared." A female voice.

Derek opened his eyes and saw one of the women staring at him.

"What did you do?" she asked.

Derek looked at Tattoo Man who was watching him closely, then turned back to the woman. He decided he probably had nothing left to lose. "B-b-bird watching," he said, "but I p-pointed my 'scope the wrong way and saw you lot."

"What will they do?"

"Th-th-think they're going to kill me."

She nodded sadly. "We are all dead. Some of us will take a long time dying."

Admitting his worst fear had made Derek's mouth dry and desolate. He remembered he still had his rucksack on his back, and it had once contained a thermos flask. He rummaged in the bag and found he still had hot tea. If he was going to die, he might as well drink his mum's tea first. The thought of her making it for him made fat tears roll down his cheeks as he sipped the hot brown liquid.

"W-want some tea?" he asked the woman, as he refilled the plastic cup.

"Yes please." She licked her lips.

"M-my mum made it for me," he said, as he reached to pass the cup across the space between them. "There's m-more... if you want to share it." He held up the flask. The woman sipped and passed the cup along. "W-where've you all come from?"

Over the next hour, the conversation kept his mind off his tragically brief future. He could hear conversations, mostly shouted into a phone in something sounding like Russian, coming from the room above. Finally, the one with the ponytail who he had learned was Dmytro, came clanging down the stairs.

"Get them to van," he said to Tattoo Man, as he opened the door and stepped outside. Derek heard the diesel engine start and a cloud of noxious black smoke puthered into the room. The women coughed as they struggled to their feet and filed out. As he stood up, Derek saw the swarthy boss man descending from the room above. He had a length of electrical cable in his hand.

"Jus' a minute, Snoopy," he said. "Hold out hands." He put his own wrists together as a demonstration. In less than a minute, Derek's wrists were bound tightly together. Tattoo Man dragged him out of the door and pushed him up into the back of the van. There was barely enough room for him to sit on the cold metal floor, perilously close to the doors. Derek had a sudden premonition of what would happen to him once the van reached the busy motorway. His hands started shaking again.

There was a whispered conversation at the back of the van, then Tattoo Man climbed in, kicking legs out of his way as he pulled the doors shut. The boss man called Danylo climbed into the passenger seat and the van set off. It hadn't travelled more than fifty yards when the brakes were jammed on making all the passengers lurch forward.

"Ebat! Politsiya!" shouted the driver, who

jumped from the van before it had stopped moving. They heard his boots crunching as he ran past. At the same moment police car sirens wailed, one of them passing close by the van's side. Tattoo Man stumbled over legs in his panic to get to the door. As it swung open he leapt out and ran towards the chain-link fence, hotly pursued by police.

Derek saw that some of the women were preparing to flee too. "D-don't run!" he said. "The police are the g-good guys. We'll all be safe now."

"For you, yes," said one young woman in a headscarf. "For me, send back to Libya and then..." she drew her finger across her throat.

"Everybody stay right where you are!" They turned to see a policeman adjusting his hat at the back of the van. The women sat down again despondently.

He looked at Derek's bound wrists. "Are you called Twitch, by any chance?" Derek smiled and nodded. "You and your friend Steven Claymore – I think you know him as Bittern? – can congratulate yourselves. We've been trying to catch this Ukrainian gang for months."

He started to untie the electric cable that held Derek's hands together. "You might even end up on the six o'clock news. How about that?" He grinned.

"It's these w-w-women should be on the news, after w-what they've all been through. They need asylum, not s-s-sending back."

"Well, that's up to immigration, not the police. But if they give evidence in court against this gang, it'll increase their chances, I'd say." He looked at the worried faces peering out of the gloom of the van. "I can't promise anything, ladies, but your ordeal at the hands of these thugs is over. Tonight you all get to sleep in a clean bed without being harassed."

Derek stared at his unfettered hands. For a brief, magical moment... they had stopped twitching.

CHAPTER 10

He Had It Coming

He had it coming. He should've known. He could've run away and hidden, but he didn't, did he? So now he was gonna get it.

"Yeah, Mr Tough Guy... can't even walk," she sneered, "Can you Tommy? Let alone run."

Fenella walked slowly around the bed where Tommy lay motionless, his eyes staring at the ceiling. She felt the weight of the dog chain, partly wrapped around the knuckles of her right fist, part lying coiled in her left hand.

"So here's what it feels like, Creep!" She swung her arm up and brought the chain swishing down through the dusty air of her bedroom. It cracked across his shins and Tommy bounced off the mattress, arms flailing. But he didn't utter a sound.

"It hurts, doesn't it, you miserable knobber?" She lashed out again, this time the chain smacking into Tommy's midriff, causing him to land on his side, doubled up.

"Think you can call me names and get away with it, don't you?" She pushed him roughly on to his back again and forced his legs down. One of Tommy's boots had come off, but Fenella ignored it.

"Yeah... 'There she goes – Wobble Thighs', 'Miss Blunderbuss', 'Fatty Fenella'." She was crying now and her nose was beginning to run. She sniffed, wiped the tears away and whacked the bed, missing his head by an inch.

"Sticks and stones will break my bones, but words will never hurt *me*." It was a rasping, hideous song.

"But they *do* fucking hurt, Tommy!" She raised her arm again. "Now you know what they feel like, you dickhead." She brought the heavy chain whipping down to land across Tommy's chest with a sickening hollow crack. He bounced once and lay motionless, his arms above his head in surrender.

Fenella sank her face into her hands, shuddering as she sobbed.

"Fenella!" Her mother's voice echoed up the stairwell. Fenella held her breath for a second. "Tea's ready!"

Fenella raised her head and shouted. "Coming,

Mum."

She dropped the chain on her worn-out Peppa Pig rug, pulled a tissue from her cardigan sleeve and wiped at the tears and snot. She left Tommy lying broken, his camouflage jacket ripped, his ammo belt twisted.

Fenella brightened as she closed her bedroom door. It was her favourite tonight – fish and chips.

CHAPTER 11

The Luxury Limo

"Travel is fatal to prejudice, bigotry, and narrow-mindedness, and many of our people need it sorely on these accounts." – Mark Twain

With these words of inspiration we'd arrived in Egypt, determined to be open-minded travellers, rather than mere tourists. The temples and tombs of Luxor would be educational for me and wife Viv, and hopefully for our 11-year-old son Michael, too. We'd never been further than northern France before, but this was 1994 and we were feeling intrepid and ready to mingle with the natives.

Having rejected the tour company's excursion offers at the hotel welcome meeting – we were too intrepid and adventurous for organised trips – we set out on foot that first morning to explore the city.

Within seconds we were mobbed by dozens of excitable, shouting men wearing galabeyas (think Wee Willie Winkie) trying to sell us everything under the sun. Kaleshes (horse and cart rides), feluccas (sailboat trips) and dozens of ancient artefacts and modern commodities were thrust upon us by a throng of desperately earnest men who simply would not take 'NO!' for an answer.

Overwhelmed by the persistent shouts and hassle from the crowd of hustlers who pursued us along the pavement, our 'mingling with the natives' had backfired spectacularly. We were about to turn and run back to the sanctuary of our hotel when a small, plump man wearing thick glasses and western clothes stepped up to us and waved all the others away.

"Don't take any notice of them. My name is Alaa and I can help you see everything you want by taking you in my car. Where would you like to go?" he asked.

We were so relieved to be rescued, we did a deal for the next three days on the spot. Alaa would take us to see the sights. His car was on the other side of the Nile, so he would meet us at our hotel after breakfast, take us across the river in a motor launch and then drive us to see the valleys of the Kings, Queens and Nobles, the tombs and the temples. We did the obligatory haggling, agreed a price and arranged to meet at 8am next day.

Alaa was waiting for us as we left the hotel's breakfast room, and escorted us to the river bank where a man with a boat was waiting. So far so good. After a ten-minute ride across the broad, brown Nile, we scrambled up the far bank to find Alaa's car… and our jaws dropped.

Once upon a time this vehicle had been a white Peugeot, but that must have been back in the time of the Pharaohs. Now it was a dented, rusty, crumpled, decrepit scrap heap with rocks wedged in front and behind all four wheels. We were aghast and stopped dead in our tracks.

"Come, come," urged Alaa, waving us towards his old wreck. "Please, sit inside and make yourselves comfortable."

After a few hearty tugs he succeeded in wrenching open a rear door and ushered Viv and Michael onto the back seat. They both looked terrified as he slammed the door shut. He then attacked the front passenger door, which emitted an anguished screech of tortured metal as it opened. With a flourish he waved me towards a seat whose red plastic cover had been split and shredded by years of harsh sunlight.

As I descended into the furnace-like interior the wrecked seat shot backwards the full length of its rail and crashed into Mike's knees, unimpeded by the latch mechanism one normally uses to adjust the position of car front seats. It didn't have one. Alaa slammed the door shut and at that moment there seemed little prospect that we'd ever get out again, dead or alive.

He then went to the front of the car, propped the bonnet up on his shoulder and fiddled about for a minute, after which there were a couple of loud clunks as the engine was cranked over in protest. A few coughs and bangs and the motor rumbled into some semblance of life, while dense smoke arose around us from an exhaust system that was more holes than pipe.

Viv, who had been sitting in stunned and wide-eyed silence, found her voice: "My God! Do you think this car is safe?"

If God replied, he couldn't be heard over the clattering engine, so I offered her my best reassurance instead. "I don't suppose there's any traffic here, and he's bound to drive slowly in this old bus. I'm sure we'll be okay." I didn't believe a word of it and the look on Viv's face told me she didn't either.

"We'll have to open a window," said Viv, as she heaved on a seized-up window winder in vain, "or we'll cook in here." Mike's side had no window handle at all, and my window was also rusted shut.

Alaa had now lowered the bonnet and was twisting two bits of wire together to hold it down. He noticed our frenzied attempts at ventilation and came to see what the problem was. I explained that we needed some air, but couldn't open the windows.

"I will open the sun roof," said Alaa, who proceeded to tug at the panel over our heads. It grudgingly moved a few inches, showering us with a blizzard of rust-flakes and dust and letting a strip of searing hot sunlight scorch my forehead.

Desperate for some leg room, Mike had pushed my seat forward with his feet until my knees crashed into the shredded remains of the dashboard, but when he relaxed my seat shot back into the rear compartment and pinned him to his seat again. With a sigh, Alaa climbed back out of the car, walked round to my side, picked up a large rock and snatched open my door.

I recoiled with a cowardly whimper, wondering if a beating with a rock was what befell all passengers who didn't sit still. But Alaa, seeing fear and panic writ large across my face, said, "My friend. It is for the seat." He proceeded to wedge the rock under my legs and – miraculously – the errant seat was fixed.

By now a crowd of small, dirty urchins in stripy galabeyas had gathered around the car. Alaa shouted some instruction to them, at which they all dashed forward, plucked the rocks from beneath the wheels (they were its brakes!) and with a graunch of gears and a cloud of smoke, Alaa urged the car into motion.

At first our Egyptian driver seemed content to potter along at 20 mph, and we started to relax as we pulled slowly away from the bank of the Nile along a strip of tarmac which threaded through a wasteland of sand and rocks. But soon he spotted a tour bus ahead, and Alaa's demeanour changed. He promptly hunched forward over the steering wheel and gunned the car's tired old engine in an attempt to get alongside the bus... just as it entered a blind bend.

We held our breath and gripped our seats with whitened knuckles as we gained speed around the long, hidden curve, expecting another vehicle to come the other way at any second. We finally pulled in front of the bus as the road straightened out. At which point Alaa relaxed, sat back in his seat and slowed back down to 20 mph again.

I looked nervously over my shoulder as the coach loomed up behind us, but at that precise moment we took a right turn to park at some huge stone monuments, so the suicidal overtaking manoeuvre had been utterly pointless.

Soon after, we were delivered to one of the more spectacular tombs where we enjoyed a leisurely visit while no fewer than four coach-loads of excursion tourists came and went in a fevered rush. They were shooed in and out with: "Ten minutes, then everyone back on the bus!"

By contrast, Alaa knew all the tomb guardians and temple officials, so we got insider info and sneak peeks into hidden side chambers that were off-limits to the general public.

After three days of being chauffeured in Alaa's Luxury Limo (always pack your sense of humour when travelling) we were feeling rather smug with our independent arrangement. We'd had an intimate insight into the lives of the ancient Egyptians, had come to enjoy his creaking old banger of a car and had even relaxed with his driving. Alaa was calm and predictable at the wheel, we realised, when compared to other Egyptian drivers.

That was when he told us we would be joining him for a meal at his home before we parted company. Our new-found confidence evaporated as we remembered our tour-rep's warning that eating outside the hotel would result in a guaranteed dose of 'Tutankhamun's revenge'. We understood it would be the height of bad manners to refuse, and as the car turned off the tourist trail and down a dusty back street, we also realised we weren't being offered a choice.

In the west bank village of Qurna, Alaa brought his rattling wreck to a halt outside a half-built house and ushered us inside. Bare concrete walls, rudimentary wickerwork beds and a solitary table appeared to be the only furniture. Small children scattered in all directions as he led us to an unlit back room that he announced was the kitchen. There, squatting in the gloom on a dirt floor, was a shy woman in a headscarf who he introduced as his wife. She was pumping a single-burner primus stove, preparing to cook us lunch.

Back in the front room, Alaa produced some chairs, spread a newspaper over the table and bade us sit. Viv was whispering in my ear that we mustn't actually eat anything when he returned with a loaf of bread baked in their outdoor oven, sliced tomatoes and homemade goats' cheese. His wife followed a few moments later with a steaming cast-iron dish full of scrambled eggs and fried onions, before lowering her eyes and backing out of the room. We sat, paralysed with uncertainty.

"Eat, *eat!*" said Alaa, as he tore off a chunk of bread and dipped into the eggs. We had no choice but to follow suit and quickly discovered this wholesome, simple fare was both delicious and filling. To our relief none of us suffered any ill-effect. We remember it to this day as a delightful taste of the real Egypt and a precious glimpse into the lives of these lovely people. Before we left, children, cousins, nephews and nieces were assembled to bid us farewell and have their photographs taken.

Seventeen years later, when Viv and I made a return visit to Luxor, we used those photos to help us track down Alaa and his family once again. The house was now completed and furnished, the little children had grown into handsome young men and women with babies of their own. And we were welcomed with a family feast – all seated on the floor around communal trays and dishes of food – to celebrate our return as long-lost friends.

Sadly, Alaa's memorable old Peugeot had coughed its last breath and been consigned to the Valley of Rust. In its place was a shiny, new-ish Nissan with electric windows and air-conditioning. Perfectly comfortable and instantly forgettable, but not a patch on the Luxury Limo.

CHAPTER 12

A Walk With God

Pamela's breath formed a vaporous cloud as she stepped into the crisp autumn morning of the Dingle Peninsula. It would, she decided, be a perfect day for a walk with God.

She shrugged on her old waxed cotton coat, grimy from years of such walks. It was clammy and cold on the outside, but the quilted tartan lining was warm and comforting and smelled faintly of her lavender perfume.

Pamela's feet were snug in multi-coloured woollen socks, but one big toe was making a bid for freedom she noticed, as she thrust her feet into muddy green wellies. That would mean more darning beside the fire later on, and a struggle to clip her thick yellow toenails, which were more difficult to reach with each passing year.

She must get going. God was impatient with her and she had a lot she wanted to tell him on the way. It was a ritual that had become important, unburdening her heart amidst the dunes, her warm words whisked away on the sea breeze. God was with her always, of course, but somehow, the fresh air and freedom of the sea strand made her thoughts spill out. He was a great listener. She could tell him anything out here, she felt, without being judged.

Soon Pamela was trudging between the marram grass tufts, feet sinking into soft sand as the froth-topped waves came into view. A flock of small birds flitted across the sea, their undersides sparkling like a shoal of silvery fish in the morning sun as they twisted and turned after their zig-zag leader.

Pamela stopped and sat on a tussock, her boots settled in the powdery sand. She called on God to come and sit with her. She liked him close so they could share the magic of the shore, sea and sky quietly together. After a couple of minutes she turned to him with loving eyes and ruffled his ears. He cocked one eyebrow expectantly and tilted his head.

"Come on now, God," she said. "Let's be gettin' home for our breakfast." He responded with an excited yelp and raced off between the dunes in the direction of their cabin, where a thin wisp of smoke trailed from the chimney.

Pamela smiled, struggled to her feet and set off after him. She didn't care what other people thought. In this remote corner of western Ireland, she knew that she and God shared a little piece of heaven.

More of Bob Goddard's work can be found at - http://www.timbuktu-publishing.co.uk/

Acknowledgements

Jennefer Rogers for unfailing encouragement, patience and advice. Also many thanks to: **Viv Goddard** for proof reading and endless cups of tea. **Matthew Hume** and **Lesley Hunt** for editing, **Jennefer Rogers, David Street** and **Linda Anne Atterton** for beta reading. **Redwell Writers** group for support and feedback.

Cover by Kayla Reese of Destiny Productions https://www.facebook.com/destinyproduct/?hc_location=ufi

About the author

Bob Goddard was born in 1953 at Holbeach in eastern England, UK. As a journalist he worked for regional and national newspapers and several magazines. Later he was editor and publisher before setting up his own marketing and distribution business. Today he writes books, short stories and occasional poetry and lives with his wife in rural Norfolk and Cyprus.

Bob's Amazon author page is at - author.to/BobGoddard

Other books by Bob Goddard

Mother Moon

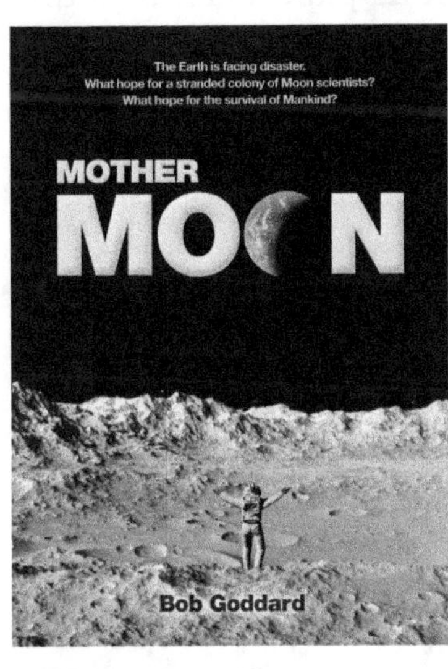

Science Fiction – Space / Historical / Sci Fi – Dystopian

Can love conquer fear in one-sixth gravity? Nadia Sokolova and Will Cooper become unlikely allies in their struggle for survival, but there are other forces at work... challenging both Moon and Earth.

2087 – A colony of scientists is stranded on the Moon as the Earth faces disaster.

1504 – A wooden sailing ship navigates the dangerous waters of religious bigotry.

Two events separated by space and time, yet destined to collide in a simple twist of fate.

Is this the end of Man - or the rebirth of Mankind?

This first in the Mother Moon series contains 336 pages of extraordinary science and conjecture to

whisk you away and blow your mind. Download the ebook now – getBook.at/MotherMoon
Or order the book in glorious paperback at a discount from the publisher – https://www.timbuktu-publishing.co.uk/
Also available via Ebay – https://www.ebay.co.uk/itm/223119242661

The Dark Side Of Mother Moon

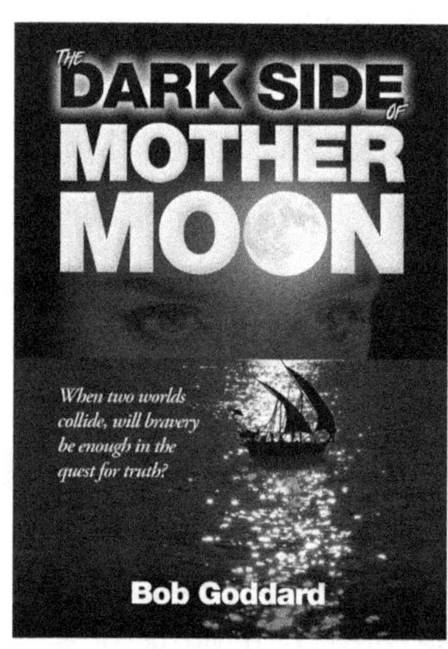

Science Fiction / Action & Adventure / Sci Fi – Dystopian
As the people of Earth uncover their astonishing origins, on the Moon a sinister secret is threatening to destroy society. Will a young man's recklessness bring the two worlds into conflict? Or can one brave woman save humanity from disaster? An awkward teenager on a wooden sailing ship and a feisty widow caught between rival Moon colonies must solve the riddle of The Dark Side Of Mother

Moon.

This sequel to Mother Moon contains 325 pages of gripping adventure to carry you across oceans of time and space. Download the ebook now – getbook.at/DarkSideMotherMoon
Or order the book in glorious paperback at a discount from the publisher – https://www.timbuktu-publishing.co.uk/
Also available via Ebay – https://www.ebay.co.uk/itm/223108942702

New Zealand Travel: Land Of The Long Wild Road

Non fiction-Memoirs & Biographes / Travel / Survivor Stories
This is an off-beat, observant and hilarious journey around New Zealand.
Bob & Viv Goddard ride two small motorcycles on gold-miner tracks, drovers' routes and Maori trails into the wilderness of this fabulous and unspoiled country.
Lured by the landscape's awesome beauty, their journey through rain forests and desert trails, up

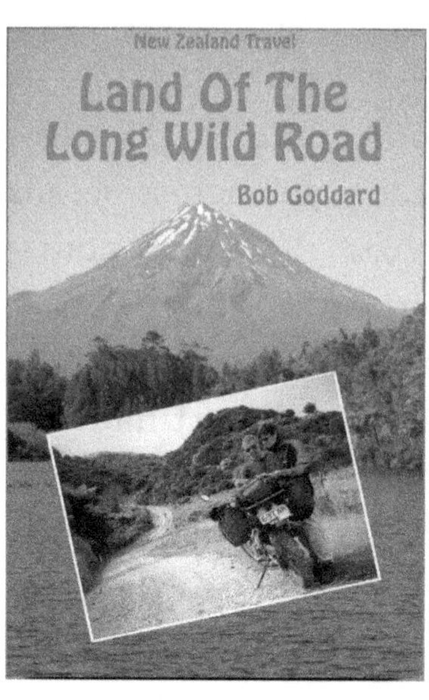

volcanoes and across river beds proves to be a life-changing experience. Hop on board for the ride of your life.

This unique and original road trip contains 258 pages of fast-paced adventure and rib-tickling humour. Download the ebook now – getbook.at/LongWildRoad

Or order the book in paperback (which contains full colour photos) at a discount from the publisher – https://www.timbuktu-publishing.co.uk/
Also available via Ebay – https://www.ebay.co.uk/itm/223056748228

Beyond Bucharest

Non fiction-Memoirs & Biographes / Travel / Survivor Stories

It sounded simple enough: copy their heroes by riding motorbikes to Eastern Europe in aid of a children's charity. But Bob & Viv Goddard were nervous

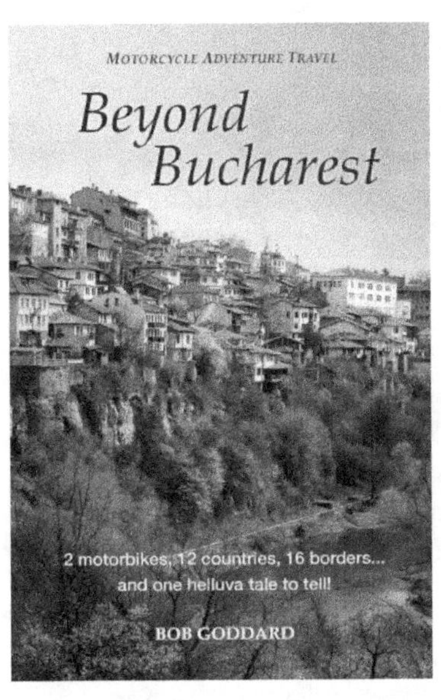

grandparents, not fit youngsters on sponsored bikes with a back-up crew.

Their ride to Bucharest and beyond, across twelve countries and sixteen border crossings, through storm, flood and tempest, was almost a challenge too far. Sixty-two people died as they battled through the wind and water. Then they realised they'd checked in for the night to a Romanian brothel...

This sequel to Land Of The Long Wild Road contains 216 pages of fast-paced adventure and rib-tickling humour. Download the ebook now – getbook.at/BeyondBucharest

Or order the book in paperback (which contains full colour photos) at a discount from the publisher – https://www.timbuktu-publishing.co.uk/

Also available via Ebay – https://www.ebay.co.uk/itm/323261835627

www.ingramcontent.com/pod-product-compliance
Lightning Source LLC
Chambersburg PA
CBHW072031170626
46811CB00008B/3030
9780956351852